MW00414449

LOVE NEVER FAILS

WRITTEN BY GINNI CONQUEST

Chapter 1 Dr. Selina Harrison

Dr. Selina Harrison, Geologist, top in her field. That's me. I've spent my adult life in the trenches traveling all over the world. I have traveled to more exotic places that people only dream of. I have traveled to oil producing countries to explain different drilling techniques that enable them to protect the Earth. That's my calling in life or I feel like it is. I want to make a difference for future generations.

One would think I had everything going for me in my life. Well, they were wrong. What they see on the outside isn't quite what it's cracked up to be. I'm sitting here at Newark Airport with my first class ticket in hand. I'm waiting to board a flight to a new beginning of my life. You see, I'm supposed to be on my honeymoon right now but I caught my fiancé, the love of my so called life, having sex with a nurse in his office. That was the last straw. I was kidding myself if I thought this was the first time that asshole did this to me but it was the first time that I actually caught him. One would think he would at least stop what he was doing due to some kind of shock of catching him in the act so to speak. But no. He seemed to enjoy that I caught him with his nurse sprawled out on top of his desk. I remember taking the ring off my finger, throwing it at him and just walking away. I was calm, I didn't yell. I felt removed from my body and mind at that point. I just needed to get the hell out of the hospital and away from this life. This was actually a blessing in disguise. She could have him.

I had turned down a job offer in Houston to work for Stone Oil Industries since I knew I was getting married and really wanted to teach at one of the colleges. When I got home, I pulled out my laptop and emailed the CEO D.P. Stone and asked him if the job was still available as things have changed with my life situation. I swear I didn't even finish hitting the "send" button when he wrote back, "When can you start?"

I remember smiling at his response even in my downward spiral of thinking about everything that I had to do. I had to pack up my apartment, send back gifts, cancel the honeymoon, the reception and church. I thought I could put my wedding dress on Ebay. So I emailed him back that I had loose ends to finish with in New Jersey and I could arrive there for July 1, get settled in over the July 4th holidays and then start on that Tuesday. The salary would make me a very wealthy woman but really, my first concern is with our environment. This CEO was a pioneer in hiring a Geologist to advise and research the different areas before drilling. I was excited about being a part of his ideology. I knew I could bring my expertise to this company and let's face it;

I needed a major change in my life. This was it. DP Stone was rolling out the red carpet for me. He said that an airline ticket would be waiting for me when I arrived at the airport. His assistant Anna would take care of all of the arrangements as well as set up a fully furnished condo close to the job. He would have a car waiting to pick me at the airport to take me to my new residence. True to his word, his assistant took care of everything for me so I didn't have to do a thing. It felt so nice to have someone take charge of my life as I felt I was really drifting but let me back track a bit.

I enlisted the help of my Mama, Maria and my best friend Julia to take care of the wedding cancellation details. I have to say that one thing going for me is my family. I'm sure there are other great things in my life but in my present state of mind, I can only think of my family. My Mama is from Spain, gorgeous with dark hair, olive skin with light eyes. Sexy and outspoken, Maria still turns heads at 65 years old. She met my Dad when he went to Spain for an archeological dig. He's also a Doctor, a Paleontologist and from Ireland. Well known in his field, Dr. Sean Harrison fell head over heels in love with Maria from the moment he saw her at the art gallery she was a curator for. Maria fell in love first with his Irish accent; I honestly don't know how they understood each other but the sparks still fly when they are in a room together. They are amazing parents, no other way to describe them. I often dreamt of finding a love like that, well, thought I had it only to discover those dreams went down the proverbial toilet. I'm a good mixture of both of them, exotic looking like my Mama yet adventurous with a scientific spirit, just like my Daddy.

So I asked Mama and Julia to take care of my

wedding dirty work and they did the job for me.
Within a week, everything was cancelled, sent
back and I even had a buyer for my wedding dress.
Now I could just concentrate on packing up my
apartment, putting some things in my parent's
attic and just moving on with my life.

Sure the asshole tried contacting me, even went as
far as to show up on my parents doorstep. That
was a big mistake. My brother just happened to
be home to check up on me and one didn't mess
with Sean Jr. My brother owned his own chain of
gyms in the Northeast so to say he's in shape and
full of muscles is an understatement. He and "The
Roc" could be brothers. The Ex couldn't get into
his car fast enough when faced with my Sean Jr.
and Mama. It was almost comical to see him drive
away with his tail between his legs. I knew he
would never bother me again.

With everything done and packed, it was the night
before I was finally leaving for Houston.

"Now sweetheart, do you have everything you
need? Money, identification, have you seen
photos of the condo where you will be living,
change over your mail mi amour?" Mama grilled

me with last minute questions.

"Yes Mama, I'm all set." I thanked them all for their support over the past month and told them I couldn't have gotten thru anything without them. We enjoyed a wonderful meal together, joked about the asshole and Mama had words of wisdom for me.

"Selina baby, someday you will meet the right man. Of that, I have no doubt. Look at your Father and me. We never thought ever we would be together and here we are. At times we can't understand each other but we have a passion for life and for each other. We know you will meet him, maybe in this new city of Houston. Keep your heart and mind open to it my baby," said Mama.

"Yeah Sis. Some cowboy or oil tycoon will help you get over that doctor really quick, if you know what I mean," laughed Sean Jr. Mama had smacked Sean Jr. across the back of his head.

"Selina doesn't need amore right now Sean, she needs time to heal. Don't think like a man but as a woman."

"I would rather my daughter take her time, do a good job for this oil company and make a name for herself in this industry. She doesn't need a man to complete her life," said Daddy. I remembered smiling over at him as he squeezed my hand. I'm definitely more like my Daddy, the adventurous type.

They dropped me off at Newark Airport this evening. I'm grateful for the evening flight as I could get some work done and maybe take a nap. I wasn't in the mood for small talk with anyone and I'm guessing the evening flight wouldn't encourage that kind of behavior.

I can't stand goodbyes so I kissed them both at the curb and headed into the airport. Promising them that I would text when I arrived, I turned towards the doors. With a big sigh, I took my first steps to an unknown future.

Walking towards the ticket counter, I planned to check in one bag and pick up my ticket, courtesy of Stone Oil Industries. I had shipped other items but figured I could buy what I needed when I arrived in Houston. Grabbing my suitcase on wheels and putting my laptop case over my shoulder, I walked up to the counter with the sense that someone was looking at me.

Sitting in one of the chairs was a gorgeous man; dark hair, blue eyes, close cropped beard and mustache: he was just staring at me. I saw his eyes travel down the length of my body and then back up to my eyes. I was mesmerized by the intensity of his stare as he seemed to look deep into my soul. I couldn't help but feel the pull of attraction to him but it wasn't something that I needed in my life right now. Hell no!

He was wearing an expensive suit; I know quality when I see it. I could also tell how built he was under that suit; I mean built all over. He wasn't as built as my brother but he was very much in shape. I saw how long his legs were as he sat there so I'm guessing he's about 6'3. He was someone who definitely commanded attention. If I wasn't so over men, he would have been someone I would have wanted to get to know and quick.

Here I am in my boyfriend jeans with low heeled pumps, white tee-shirt wearing a jean jacket. My dark brown hair was in waves past my shoulders. I wondered what his perusal was all about.

Frowning at him in annoyance with the hope to discourage him, I turned my attention back to the ticket agent. I was not in the mood for the opposite sex; that much was for sure.

"Hi, I'm Dr. Selina Harrison. I'd like to pick up my ticket please." Glancing in the direction of that handsome man again, I saw him give me a little smirk of his lips. How annoying. I slammed my ID a little harder on the counter than I should have. Why did I even look back at him? This man was definitely getting on my last nerve. I don't need this right now. I watched as the ticket agent punched in my name and still felt that man staring at me. I was thinking of asking him what his problem was but I didn't want to invite a conversation with him. I was done with men, no matter what they looked like.

"Here's your First Class ticket Dr. Harrison, are you checking that bag?"

"Yes please. I'll take the laptop with me to get some work done."

"Ok, we will be boarding first class passengers in a few moments. Enjoy your flight Doctor."

"Thank you." Heading over to one of the chairs, I made sure to steer clear of the intense looking man that still focused his attention on me.

Chapter 2 DP Stone

The minute she walked into the waiting area, I couldn't keep my eyes off of her. I'm thinking she has to be Spanish; maybe half with her dark brown hair, topaz colored eyes and olive like complexion. Watching her walk in with those pumps and jeans, I was at least happy to know she was going to Houston. The thought of her legs wrapped around me wearing those pumps stuck in my mind. She caught me staring at her, like she knew what I was thinking about. When she frowned at me, she became a challenge. The gauntlet was thrown down. At my age, we are done with the bullshit, well; we have a different type of bullshit to deal with. I know what I want when I see it. There is no second guessing. When I set my mind to something, I never fail; whether in business or affairs of the heart. This was one woman I wanted. I caught myself thinking about the reasons why she was going to Houston; for work, a man, a woman, hey you never know nowadays. But no, it had to be for work. She seemed like she was running from something to a new beginning. I was good at reading people; I had to be as CEO at my job. I felt a little guilty trying to listen to her conversation with the ticket agent. I am happy to hear she is in First Class as I am. Maybe if the love god's would allow it, she would be sitting next to me. I can only hope. Then I hear her name: Dr. Selina Harrison. Oh my God, my new employee! You have got to be kidding me! Now the love god's are turning against me. Then I remembered the date. It's July 1, the day that Dr. Harrison agreed to come to Houston. Of course my assistant would have us booked on the same flight. For a brief second, I thought that I wouldn't speak to Dr. Harrison or if I did, never divulge who I am. Now that would cause a major problem when she showed up to work after July 4th. Not a good way to start. No, I will be upfront and honest with her if I have the chance to have a conversation with her or if the situation warranted it.

I watched as she took a drink from her bottled water. I couldn't help looking at her full lips on that bottle as her gorgeous neck bent back slightly as she drank. Oh God, what is wrong with me? I imagined what her lips would be like on my, ok now is not the time to think about that. Hearing her cell phone ring, she looked down at her it and smiled. As she answered the phone, I noticed her delicate hands and that her ring finger was bare. Speaking in Spanish, I was right about her nationality. If Dr. Harrison wasn't one of the most beautiful women I have ever seen, then call me blind. We would definitely get to know each well, to Hell with the job.

Hearing over the speaker the call to board First Class passengers, I let her go first while I pretended to answer an email on my Iphone. I wanted to see where she was sitting. I had a feeling she would be sitting next to me since my assistant Anna arranged the flight. Ok, my turn to board the plane.

Just my luck. My eyes find her exactly where I wanted her; in the seat next to me. I have at least five hours of flight time sitting next to this gorgeous princess. I made a mental note to give a nice bonus to my assistant.

"Excuse me; I believe this is my seat."

"Oh, I'm sorry, let me move this for… you." I noticed her eyes grow a darker almost caramel color as she looked up at me. I also noticed how she breathed the word "you" after a brief second. Taking her laptop from my seat, she looked away but not before I saw her glance down my body right down to my shoes. My senses picked up an attraction from her but she was fighting it. I wanted her, plain and simple. When I set my mind to something, I rarely lose. But this woman, she is a mystery that I planned to find out about.

"My name is Damien. Is this your first time in Houston?"

"I'm Selina. Yes, I'm going to be living there for business, at least for the next year." Princess didn't look at me but was fidgeting with her laptop, trying to get a connection.

"Damn this thing, just when I need to get a jump start on work." She said that more to herself than to me. Seeing her reach up to press the button for the flight attendant, I noticed how her tee-shirt stretched across her generous breasts and her small waist. I already know that she was curvy in the hips and about 5'4. I'm guessing a dynamo personality, maybe a slight temper. I plan on finding out.

I saw the flight attendant come right over to us. That's the beauty of First Class, wonderful service.

"How may I help you?"

"Two things, will there be wifi on this flight? And may I get a drink please?"

"That sounds good," I added. "What are you having?"

"A vodka cranberry to start," Selina answered.

"A Corona for me with lime would be great."

"Ok, I'll be right back with your drinks and the wifi password. You will have to wait until we get to cruising speed before logging on though."

"Thank you," said Selina.

"I also have some nice appetizers that I will bring the both of you. Will that be all Mr. and Mrs.?"

"Oh God no," laughed Selina. "We aren't married or even together."

"Well, you should be; such a handsome couple. I'm sorry if I embarrassed you." I noticed that the flight attendant took her time looking at me the minute she knew Selina and I was not a couple. Sorry, you are not the one I'm interested in.

"Its fine," answered Selina. As the flight attendant walked away, I waited until she was out of earshot from us.

"I have to agree with her, you are gorgeous." I couldn't help myself; I wanted to see how far I could push her. Seeing the color creep up into her cheeks, she barely whispered thank you and turned her eyes away. I felt that she shut herself down and did not want to engage a conversation with me.

So I decided to get comfortable for the flight. Standing up, I took off my suit jacket and laid it flat in the overhead compartment. The tie came off next and joined the jacket. I saw her slide a glance towards me to see what I was doing. Sitting back down, I undid my cuff buttons and rolled my sleeves up to my elbow. The tattoo of an eagle was emblazoned on my forearm from my military days. I noticed that she was glancing at it and also at what I was doing. I undid a few of the shirt buttons and felt that I could relax on this flight now. Grabbing my laptop, I would get some work done on the long flight home while planning my strategy in getting to know this princess. There was no doubt the attraction was there between us and I planned on doing something about it.

Chapter 3   Selina

Ok this is not happening! I can't believe I'm attracted to this gorgeous man sitting next to me. After my ruined relationship, I should be turned off by men. My head is telling me to stay away, but my heart is bouncing out of control as well as other parts of my body. The quicker we get to Houston, the easier it will be to move on with my life, pure and simple. Yet I'm not having pure thoughts right about this time. By saying a Hail Mary, maybe she will help me get thru this flight and fight all temptation. It's not working, the prayer I mean. I need a drink. Can you sense my panic?

Now why is he getting out of his seat? Just a small glance to my right and I see him taking off his jacket and tie. Oh God, I was right; not only tall but he is built, not like the asshole. I have got to stop comparing the two of them. As Damien sat back down, I look over at him and give him a shy smile as I saw his eyes look right into my soul.

Seeing a tattoo on his muscular forearm just about does me in. Oh my God a tattoo! Get a grip Selina. You are turned off from the male sex right now. I keep telling myself this. They are too much trouble. Where is that drink?

"Selina, are you ok?"

"Yes, just wondering where our drinks are." That lie came out a little too quickly from my lips. Damien narrowed his eyes and leaned in towards me.

"Be honest with yourself: is that what you are really thinking about as you are sitting here next to me?"

I felt my heart jump in my chest at his direct words to me. Trust me, that wasn't the only part of me being affected by him. I felt that unmistakable longing for love, for complete satisfaction from a man to a woman. It was getting a little uncomfortable sitting next to him as my body and mind were betraying me but I forced myself to have a calm demeanor even though I was quivering on the inside.

Given a reprieve of having to answer, the flight attendant came over with our drinks.

"After we get to cruising altitude, I'll have food to serve the both of you. In the meantime, relax and make sure your seat belts are fastened. We are getting ready to take off."

Looking for my other seat belt buckle, I realize it's tangled up with the gorgeous hunk. This can't be happening.

"Umm, I believe that part of the buckle is mine."

"Well, let's get this figured out then, shall we?"

Putting his Corona down on the floor next to him, I could tell he was starting to enjoy every minute of this. He reached over to my other side and pulled the belt across my waist. For a brief second, his forearm brushed against my breast which caused me to suck in my breath. I can't believe he is doing this.

"I think I can take care of this now," I told him. Totally ignoring me, Damien's head was bent over by my face. The smell of his cologne was an aphrodisiac to me as it tantalized my senses. I was able to get a good look at him, even down to his dimples thru his close cropped beard that I imagined he has if I could get him to smile on this trip. Pulling the other side from in between our seat, he clicked the belt and tightened it around me. Glancing at me as his mouth was barely inches from my lips, time seemed suspended between us. His eyes devoured my lips and then reached up to my eyes, darkening with desire as he stared at me. I could feel him without him touching me. How is that possible?

"Thank you," I whispered. With a slight smirk, he sat back in his chair. Taking a deep swig of his beer that was the only telltale sign that showed he was as attracted to me as I was to him. Maybe a quick fling was what I needed to make me get over the asshole as well as take away my insecurity of not being pleasing to a man. Maybe it was the asshole that wasn't good in bed. I really didn't have much to compare him to. My friend Julia always said I needed to go out and just have fun, one night stands, see what was out there. Maybe my upbringing stopped me from having that kind of fun as my Catholic roots always took a firm hold on me. Being raised in a Spanish and Irish home, I didn't stand a chance. Maybe this time, I can relax the rules just a bit for this man.

The flight attendant made the announcement over

the PA system that we were next in line to leave. I felt my anxiety kick up a bit. I finished my drink in two big gulps as the vodka hit my stomach like a ton a bricks. The warmth of it spread throughout my body. As I looked out the window, I felt a tear fall down my cheek and then another and another. I can't lose it in front of this man but I couldn't help myself. I was leaving devastation behind to living in an unknown city and carrying a broken heart. Feeling a hanky pressed into my hand, I glanced down at it and saw the monogram emblazoned on it: DS. I couldn't look at him but just nodded my head as I used the hanky to wipe the tears from my cheeks as I continued to look out the window. A warm hand held onto mine which made my emotions come bubbling to the surface. Just his kind gestures put me over the top. I just let the tears fall as soft sobs shook my body as the plane lifted us into the air and towards my new life.

Chapter 4 Damien

She was killing me. Hearing the sobs leave her body, this was more than just the flight. I know her resume, she traveled all over the world; it's not the flight. No, this was heartbreak, pure and simple or maybe not so simple. Whoever he was that broke her heart was a fucking loser in my mind.   Holding her hand seemed to make her sobs worse but I didn't want to let her go. I couldn't. We'll get to cruising altitude; get us another drink and something to eat. Maybe she will open up but something tells me she won't. At least this will help her; a good cleansing cry didn't hurt anyone and helped set them on the right path to rediscovery.

As the plane leveled off, she pulled her hand from mine and apologized for losing it like she did.

"It's fine Princess. I'm glad to have been here to help."

"Princess? Hardly."

"If you were mine, you would definitely be my Princess. May I?"

Giving me a slight nod, I reached over to brush the tears from her cheeks as she just stared at me. Licking her lips, I just stared at the fullness of the bottom lip. I reached over and touched it with my thumb as I felt her tremble a bit from just that light touch. I felt it right down to my crotch. For the first time ever, I recognized this woman had the power to bring me to my knees. I have never felt this protective over a woman before and I've had many that have come in and out of my life. No one made me react like Selina has.

The flight attendant came over just at this moment with a tray of food and another vodka cranberry and a Corona.

"You can use the wifi now. Just press the button overhead if you need anything else."

"Thank you," said Selina.

Raising her glass to mine, Selina made a toast.

"Here's to new beginnings, both personal and business."

"That sounds good to me Princess."

Looking at me, Selina took a big sip of her second drink. Laying sideways in her seat, she tipped it back a little and settled in comfortably with her legs tucked up under her.

"I was supposed to be on my honeymoon right now. I cancelled our wedding a month ago after I found him screwing a nurse in his office when I stopped by unexpectedly. I can't get that vision out of my head and really in my heart know it wasn't the first time he cheated on me. It was the first time I caught him and that was that. I guess I can count myself lucky that I found out before we got married."

"That man is an asshole. You need to find the right man who will treat you the way you should be treated."

Selina laughed out loud. "Really Damien, you guys are all the same. Get in and get out."

"Not all men sweetheart, you just haven't met the right one." I reached out to the curve of her cheek and brushed my fingers down her face and onto her neck. Reaching behind her neck, I pulled her closer to me as I met her halfway. I had to kiss her, had to show her that she was partially in control while I was totally in control of her.

"I want to kiss you Princess."

Feeling the slight nod of her head, I brought my lips to hers. Feeling her hands on my shirt, she pulled me closer while her lips parted for me. Slanting my mouth against hers, my lips were hot as they had their first taste. Hearing a soft moan come deep within her throat, our tongues were entwined with each other, devouring each other. I was lost in her. This was dangerous. I explored her mouth, my hand taking some liberty in moving lower down her neck to slightly inside her shirt. When she arched her back into me, feeling her breasts on my chest was totally sexy. Hearing the sounds coming from her made my dick react. All I could say was her fiancé was an idiot to give this woman up. I can only imagine what she would be like in bed but knew that we had to slow this up before things got out of control. Then I felt her hand travel down the front of my shirt. She slowly unbuttoned more of the top buttons as her mouth traveled down my neck and onto my chest. Jesus, what was she doing to me? I quickly looked around, thankful we were in the last seats and First Class wasn't full either. Since it was evening, the cabin lights were already muted so that added to mood.

As her hand drifted down onto my lap, I had to stop her.

"Hold that thought Princess."

I stood up and grabbed two blankets from the overhead compartments as Selina brought both of our seats to lay back. Sitting back down next to her, I put the blankets on top of us.

"What do you want Selina?"

"I want to forget."

"Lower your jeans now."

Selina kept her eyes focused on mine as I saw her movement under the blanket.

"Lower your panties now."

She nodded her head and looked at me, her topaz eyes turning a darker shade from lust.

"I'm going to make you forget all about him, make no doubt about that."

As I lay on my side, my fingers found what I have been thinking about all night and pushed right into her. Hearing her moan out loud, I covered her lips with mine. I stopped moving my fingers and moved my mouth to her ear.

"You can't do that, bite my shoulder when you come but you can't moan out loud like that here. Do you understand me?" Nodding her understanding, I felt her shift closer to my fingers.

"Tell me what you want Selina."

"I want you to make me come Damien, I want to forget, please."

"My pleasure ma'am." Sliding my fingers up and down her folds, I parted them with my hand while my mouth was on hers. She spread her legs as far as she could in the seat as I stuck two fingers deep within her. She actually was biting my tongue as she kept her moan quiet like I instructed her. As waves of pleasure started building within her, I knew she was close by how she was gripping my fingers inside of her. Her hips started moving against my fingers as my thumb rubbed against her clit. She was coming apart in my arms as she buried her face in my neck and bit down as her whole body shuttered from this experience. Wave after wave of pleasure came crashing down on her as I didn't let up until I felt her quiet down from her orgasm. Pulling my fingers from her, I lifted my hand to my mouth to lick my fingers while watching her.

"Oh my God," she whispered.

"Taste." Selina licked my fingers, sucking them right into her mouth which sent shock waves right into my dick.

Pulling my fingers from her mouth, she moved her hand under the blankets right to the zipper of my

pants. As she unzipped my pants, she kept her
eyes locked onto mine. Giving me a sly smile, she
went down under the blanket and pulled my pants
down.   My dick had a mind of its own and it
wanted Selina. Feeling light kisses up and down
the length of me, she licked the whole top part
before I pushed myself into her mouth. Feeling
the vibration of her moan on me made me put my
head back into my seat as Selina made love to me.
Moving her hand up and down the length of it as
her mouth and tongue were sucking, it was an
amazing feeling. As she cupped my balls, I knew
that I was going to come in her mouth sooner than
later. I always like to be in control of these
situations but was fast loosing myself in Selina.
Feeling her nails rake over my length, she
concentrated on the tip before engulfing it all into
her mouth and towards the back of her throat.
Reaching under the blanket, I held her head in
place while I fucked her mouth. I made sure that I
didn't push too hard to hurt her but just enough to
give her what we both wanted. Feeling the rush
starting, I jerked as I released myself within her
hot mouth. As my spasms subsided, Selina came

out from under the blanket and smiled at me. She placed a kiss on my cheek and whispered a thank you in my ear.

"There's plenty more where that came from Princess." Not liking how she looked at me, it seemed that she was making this a one night stand. She was definitely in for a rude awakening. At that moment, I decided to keep my association with her a secret. She would know that I always got what I wanted and I was just starting with her.

Chapter 5 Selina

I knew the minute he offered me his hand and hanky, I wanted to have some kind of sex with him; Damien would be my one night stand. What were the chances we would ever see each other again? I decided to consume a bit more alcohol to give myself some courage and gave him signs that I would be open to consensual adult sex. How clinical that sounded but I really needed to forget the asshole and see if I was attractive to the opposite sex. It seemed like Damien was into me too so what the hell. I decided to tell him what happened to me. Getting all comfy, I related the story of how I found my fiancée screwing that tramp and that I reached out to the new boss to see if the job was still available in Houston. Damien just understood everything. He was so easy to talk to.

When he reached out to me, I was a goner. I'm so glad he made the first move as I really didn't know how I was going to initiate anything. At a club was one thing; an airplane I was lost. Moving closer to him, I wanted his lips on mine so badly. I knew he would help me on the road to forget my heartbreak. I felt a little guilty using him but I was attracted to him. He was a warm, attractive man that knew what he was doing; he seemed a bit of a domineering alpha male type but that was fine with me. I didn't have the experience I knew he had so that helped make this easier. It would be exciting to give control to him. I just didn't want to get caught but it seemed like everyone was asleep and First Class wasn't even sold out. Lucky us.

As I started to moan deep in my throat, he warned me to be quiet so we didn't get caught. That would be mortifying but made it all the more risqué. So grabbing a few blankets and putting the seats down, I was already shaking with excitement on this sexy adventure, knowing that this man was just what I needed right at this moment. He would be the one to initiate the new me.

When he ordered me to take my jeans and panties off, a flood of excitement reached my core. As he fingers buried themselves in me, I was transported to another realm, where new beginnings began and nightmares ended.   Doing what he told me to do, I kept my face in his neck and bit down as I came hard against his fingers. I never had this reaction with the asshole before so I know the healing process had begun. Then I couldn't wait to give him the same pleasure back.

I was told that I wasn't good at oral sex but maybe it was the man that I was with.

Damien couldn't get enough of what I did to him; it gave me a sense of power and accomplishment, especially when he came in my mouth. He was more endowed than what I've known too and was definitely attracted to me judging by his response. That much I know.

I wanted to shout for joy that I did it, that I made

another man feel as wonderful as he made me feel. I took everything that Damien gave me and tried not to have any type of connection with him. It wouldn't work if I developed any type of feelings for him. That would be my undoing. I had to stay strong and just concentrate on my new job. But first I had to get thru the rest of this flight. So I settled back in my seat and thought about getting some work done. Feeling good about myself, I thought I was a bit of a vixen but in reality, it needed to be coaxed out of me. This man definitely did that for me. Just looking at him made me want to do things that I've never done and only read about. So I told him thank you and tried to dismiss him a bit. I wanted to distance myself from him. No sense in getting caught up in him if this was a onetime thing. Seeing the look in his eyes scared me as he seemed to tell me that he was nowhere near done with me. What are the chances that we would meet up again anyway? Houston was a big city.

I was able to get a wifi password hook up and got to work on mapping the new drilling site for Stone Oil Industries. I kept my conversation to a minimum with Damien; I got what I wanted from him, now it was time for me and for healing. But maybe, I will give him my number. He could be my "friend with benefits" if he would be agreeable to that. This is a new Selina taking control over her life. I actually started getting excited about the new me.

Chapter 6 Damien

So Selina is keeping her distance. That's ok; I'll have the last laugh come Tuesday. She never asked me what I did for a living. I never asked her either to keep my part a secret. Knowing that I would see her again made what would have been a bit of panic take a back seat to the excitement of getting to know her. We finished off the appetizers and had one more round of drinks. She seemed very pleased with herself as she started some of the work for me on her laptop. That brought a smile to my face. I realized I had to do one thing so reaching into my pocket, I grabbed my cell phone and typed a quick text to my driver who was waiting for me.

DT, you will be driving Dr. Harrison to her apartment. Do not under any circumstances acknowledge me at all. I will not be riding with her. She has no idea who I am and I want to keep it that way until Tuesday morning. I will take a cab to my condo.

Boss, your secret is safe with me. I will enjoy ignoring you, BUT you will never take a cab on my watch. I will have my friend Larry pick you up in his sedan. He will be holding a sign with your last name on it. It's not safe for you to take a cab.

DT, you are the best. A smart ass but the best. Thank you. We should be landing in about an hour. I trust you can get your friend there in time?

Yes Boss, already text him. He will be waiting for you when you walk out of baggage claim. If he sees the doctor with you, he will discreetly move the sign away. Just look for a white rose in his lapel.

DT, a white rose?

Yes Boss, he says it's his signature style, gets the ladies all the time.

Well, it won't have an effect on me but at least I will know who he is. Thanks DT.

See you Tuesday Boss. Let me know if you need a driver over the weekend. If not, I'll pick you up on Tuesday at 7am as usual. Happy 4th.

Happy 4th to you too DT.

Ok, so that was taken care of. Since I'm getting ignored by Princess Selina, I'll close my eyes for a few minutes until we start to descend. I can start to plot and plan how I will win her over.

Chapter 7 Houston

"Damien, we are getting ready to land." I looked at this formidable man as he slept. His eyelashes were so long, they were the kind that women would be jealous of. Looking at his mouth and hands, I had already known firsthand what he was capable of. I decided to give him my cell number. It would be nice to have a "friend" in Houston. When I looked back up to his face, he was staring right at me. I was lost in those blue depths and really couldn't gage what he was thinking about. "We are getting ready to land. You were sleeping for the last hour."

"What were you doing while I was sleeping?" Of course he guessed I was looking at him from time to time. Who wouldn't? He was gorgeous. "I got a good head start on work for my new job. Wrote a few emails, made up lists of what I would need for my new home, that kind of thing."

"I understand. Would it be too presumptuous of me to ask for your number? I would love to see you again Selina, once you get settled in. I could show you around Houston to get you acquainted with the area."

"I would love that Damien." Reaching into my bag, I grabbed one of my cards. "Here's my cell on my geologist business card. I start at my new job on Tuesday and will know after that day how my hours will be. I also want to thank you for your kindness towards me on this flight. I appreciate it."

"It was my pleasure Princess. I look forward to seeing you again and sharing some more kindness with you."

As I felt the redness creep into my cheeks, I sensed he was going to say something else to me. Just then, the plane touched down and I needed to gather my belongings. To say that I wasn't thinking about what we shared on this flight would be a total lie. I really hoped he would contact me but if he didn't, I could remember my flight adventure with a smile. When I was ready to exit the plane, Damien stood and let me out of the seat first. As I felt the heat of his body radiate towards me, my body reacted to how close he was. I could still smell his cologne. Closing my eyes for a second, I yelled at myself to stop acting like a sex crazed woman. I was trying to be sophisticated about the whole experience but was failing miserably. Feeling Damien put his face down to my ear, I felt his breath.

"Are you ok?"

Shaking myself out of my thoughts, I actually did a little jump as I didn't expect him to say anything to me. I heard him chuckle deep in his throat and felt him brush lightly up against me.

"Yes Damien. I'm fine. I just sat a little too long."

Heading towards baggage claim, Damien walked next to me. He reached for my laptop to carry it for me. God, he was totally the type of man I loved. I smiled up at him to thank him again for his kindness. He knew that I was anxious at starting my new life and just wanted to help me while he could. Coming off the escalator, I saw my driver holding the sign with my name on it.

"Well Damien, this is where I'm going. I see my driver right over there."

"And my driver is over there Princess. Here's your laptop. Good luck with your new job and I'll call you next week to get together." He leaned down to kiss me on the cheek. His cologne lingered on me when he pulled away. Looking into his eyes, I already missed him and he didn't even walk away yet. This was ridiculous.

"See you soon." I walked over to meet my driver.

"I'm Dr. Harrison."

"Welcome to Houston Dr. Harrison. My name is DT. How many bags do you have?"

"I just have one to collect."

"Ok, let's go and pick it up." DT tipped his hat in my direction and gave me a big welcoming smile. I looked in the direction to where Damien walked and didn't see him anywhere. Oh well, I will most likely not be seeing him again anyway. I didn't get his number so if he doesn't call me, he will be a wonderful memory that I will have. I really didn't need complications in my life right now anyway. That's what I tried to tell myself. But wow. What a man! With my luck, he is probably married. I didn't see a ring on his finger, but that didn't mean a thing nowadays. I didn't even think about that until now. Nothing I could do about it now anyway.

Moving forward with DT, the luggage was already going around the belt. Thankfully, my bag was one of the first ones that came off the plane and then we were on our way to the car.

Making our way to the parking lot, I noticed that DT escorted me right to a limo parked by the curb. How nice of DP Stone to send such a nice car to bring me to my new condo. I could definitely get used to this treatment. DT held opened the door for me and then stowed my luggage in the trunk. Hearing my cell ring, I looked at the call coming in. My heart fell a little that it wasn't a Houston number that could be Damien but was my Mama. "Hola Mama." I felt it was so much faster to speak to my Mama in Spanish. It also gave me good practice too. Launching into explaining that the flight was just fine and that I arrived, I assured her that I would contact her over the weekend to let her know that I'm settling in just fine. Catching DT looking at me in the rearview mirror, I ended the phone call so I could look around the scenery as we drove thru the different neighborhoods.

"Sorry DT. I had to take that call."

"That's fine Dr. Harrison. Are you Spanish?"

"Yes, Spanish and Irish. It's easier to get my thoughts across to Mama in her native language."

"I understand that. My family is Spanish too and it's the same thing. I'll take you to your condo now. It's in a complex right near the company. I have a packet that I've been instructed to give you. It has your key card to your condo and a key card to get thru security on Tuesday morning. I will be picking you up at 8am to bring you to the office. If you want, you can even walk to work but I'll be at your disposal. If I'm not available, Jose will be your driver. My primary job is to drive Mr. Stone. Is this your first time in Houston?"

"Yes, it is. I'm excited about this new job and what it entails."

"I'm sure you will do an amazing job Dr. Harrison. Mr. Stone expressed his pleasure about you joining his company. He's really innovative in this business."

"How long have you worked for him?"

"Since he took over; about 5 years now."

Looking out the window, Selina looked at the different neighborhoods and the stores they passed.

"Is there a grocery store that is nearby the complex that I could go to? I need to pick up some groceries to get me thru the weekend."

"Yes, there is, within walking distance. Everything is in the packet. However, Mr. Stone's assistant stocked up the fridge with basics for you: fruits, vegetables, milk, bread, a roasted chicken too. He spared no expense to have you here Dr. Harrison."

"Please call me Selina."

"Will do Selina. And here we are."

Driving up to the gates and a security guard, DT informed the guard who I was. Rolling down the window, I introduced myself to the guard as he welcomed me to the complex. Waving us thru, DT drove me to my section of the complex and helped me out of the car. I stood there looking around at my surroundings. It was a beautiful stone building that had a water fountain in the circle of the driveway. It was all lit up this evening. It was definitely an expensive complex. I was excited to see what my condo looked like. Coming back over to me with my suitcase, DT handed the folder to me and the key to my condo.

"Here you go Selina. It's everything you need. The office is right over there, the big towering one."

"Which floor is the company?"

"The whole building is Stone Oil Industries. Welcome to Houston where everything is on a larger scale. Here is my card. Call if you need anything. I'll see you at 7:45am on Tuesday. Oh and Selina, Happy July 4th."

"You too DT. Thank you for everything. Oh and what does DT stand for?"

"Don Tomas. Buenos noches Senorita." As he drove off, I took a deep breath and walked into the building. Noticing that I was on the 14th floor, I stepped into the elevator with a bit of excitement building inside of me. Reaching the 14th floor, I looked at the number on the key card. Number 1440. Walking that way, I found my door and slipped the card in it. Hearing the click, I opened the door, turned on the lights and my heart stopped at how beautiful the place was. I realized I walked in with my mouth open and just let the door shut behind me. Placing the key card on the counter, I left my bag by the front door and walked into the room. I couldn't believe how amazing this place was. Wall to wall windows which overlooked a beautiful lake was breathtaking. The lake had lit up aerator fountains in it. There was a deck outside the sliding doors that I could sit and relax in the evenings. In the living room, there was a flat screen TV with a sectional couch facing it. It was plush and it looked like it would hug me back when I sat in it.

Running my hand down the granite counter top, the kitchen was a dream to cook in. I only hoped I would have time to do it justice. I loved to cook and did so at every opportunity I had.

Walking down the hall, I found a room that was set

up to be my office. It had my new work laptop there as well as books and information about Stone Oil Industries. It had everything I could possibly need at my disposal. Walking across the hall was my new bedroom. With a four poster king size bed and the same gorgeous view of the lake, I was shocked at how generous my new boss was. The master bathroom had a sunken Jacuzzi tub, a shower, all in marble. I just sat on the bed totally in shock as a text came thru. I didn't recognize the number but had a feeling it was from D.P. Stone.

Dr. Harrison, DT just text me that he has dropped you off at your new condo and gave you the instruction packet.

Yes, thank you Mr. Stone. I have everything.

I trust your condo is to your liking.

Yes, quite beautiful and unexpected. Thank you.

Well, I'll see you on Tuesday morning then. Now you have my text if you need anything over the weekend. Happy 4th Dr. Harrison. Welcome to Houston.

Thank you Mr. Stone. See you on Tuesday.

Now that was a nice welcome. It was time to get situated and just relax. I noticed the boxes that I shipped were all stacked in the corner. Thank God. They mostly contained my suits for work, my clothes for working in the field and some cocktail dresses just in case. I'll call Julia and get her up to speed. She isn't going to believe this place. I'll take some photos first so I can email them to her as well as to my parents.

Chapter 8 Damien

I noticed where DT was the minute we got off the escalator. He caught my eye and motioned with his head to where his friend was. Seeing the white rose in Larry's lapel, I gave DT a smirk to acknowledge that I saw his friend. Looking down at Selina, I gave her a kiss goodbye on her cheek and watched her walk over to DT. The sexy sway of her hips caught my eye. She was all woman:

brilliant, sexy and gorgeous all wrapped up in one. I had a feeling that Tuesday would be a mess dealing with her but it was so worth what happened on the plane. I definitely wanted to see more of Dr. Harrison, that was a given. I would take my chances. I blended into the crowd as I walked over to Larry.

"Mr. Stone?"

"Yes Larry. Thank you for picking me up."

"Where to Mr. Stone."

"My place on Sunset."

"Yes Sir. This way to the car." So glancing at Selina one more time, I left with Larry to head on home. I figured that DT would text me after he dropped her at the condo. I would then give her about 10 minutes to explore the place and then text her.

I started to think of what her reaction would be on Tuesday at the staff meeting. I think I could safely say that it wouldn't be good. Smiling to myself, I knew that it was worth it. As we drove out of the airport, I couldn't help but think about Selina. I knew I had my hands full the minute her lips touched mine. This is someone that could ruin me. I recognized that immediately. Now the flight; I knew it was definitely something she normally wouldn't do, especially now at this time of her life. And I definitely wasn't planning on being a rebound relationship. It sounded like she was settling anyway with her fiancée. She was just so damned sexy as she came apart in my arms. I put my head against the back of the seat. When her lips moved on my…

"Excuse me Mr. Stone. Which complex is it?"

"Sorry Larry, I wasn't paying attention. The last one on the right."

Reaching into my wallet for my key card, I also pulled out a hundred to give to Larry.

"Thanks Larry. Happy 4th."

"Thank you Mr. Stone. Same to you."

I opened the door myself as Larry jumped out of the car. I hated that drivers felt that they needed to do that for me. I had stopped DT from doing that year's ago. He insisted that when there was a dinner or a black tie function that I needed to attend, he would open the door for me as it was proper. I grudgingly conceded to that and as time went forward, that made sense. With the newspaper photographers always snapping photos at these events, DT loved doing that part of his job. He was very important to me and I made sure to take care of him and his family.

Putting the key card in my door, I flipped on lights and thought home sweet home. I usually hated coming back to my place after a trip. Sometimes I missed having a wife and kids to come home to. It's what I should have in my life but my job was my life. Who was I kidding? I didn't meet anyone that I wanted to share my life with until now. Putting my bag on the counter, I needed a cup of coffee to keep me going for a bit as I needed to catch up on emails.

I promised myself that I would relax this weekend. I had a choice of a few BBQ's to go to. I figured I would go to my Vice President's family outing tomorrow. I went to college with Steve Miller and loved his family. His mom was after me to settle down. I always told her that when I met the right woman, she would be the first to know. She was as bad as my mom. And that reminded me; I had to see my family on Sunday. Let the grilling begin. Dad always had a million and one questions about the new drilling and now had questions about our new geologist. I made him retire 5 years ago to take my mom on trips and to enjoy his life. I had plans for Stone Oil Industries to take it into the next decade. Dad knew it was time to give me the reins to take over and I didn't look back.

A text was coming in that brought me out of my thoughts. Seeing it was DT, I read that he dropped Selina off and gave her the instruction packet I wanted her to have. I'll give her a few minutes to look at her place and then I'll text her.

Adding milk and sugar to my coffee, I leaned into the counter.

Dr. Selina Harrison, you have met your match. Opening my phone, I searched for her cell number that I had already in my phone. Sending her a text to see if everything was good at the condo, I knew she would be pleased with her living arrangements. I smiled as I saw her reply. Enjoy your holiday weekend Selina. I'll see you on Tuesday.

Chapter 9 Happy July 4th

I stretched as I opened my eyes to the sunlight filling my bedroom. At first I forgot where I was and then smiled at my new surroundings. Jumping out of bed, I turned on the shower and just stood there with the water beating down on me. I was excited as today I would finish unpacking but first I needed to go shopping.

It was July 4th weekend. Maybe this town would have fireworks that I could go to. I always loved to see the colors burst overhead. It just seemed like the appropriate way to celebrate this country's birthday.

Finishing up, I checked the weather on the news station and saw it was a hot one. Digging out a sundress, I dried my hair, put on a little mascara and lip gloss. Finding my little flats, I went into the kitchen to see what Anna picked up for me. I grabbed an apple, a piece of cheese and some juice. I was excited to see what this town had to offer.

Heading to the elevator, I saw a few people that wished me a Happy 4th and I said it back to them.

Everyone seems friendly enough. Putting on my sunglasses, I braced myself for the hot Houston sun. I thought it was bad enough in New Jersey but this was even hotter. I figured I would get used to it as time went on.

Waving hello to the security guard, I introduced myself but they already knew who I was. I asked about fireworks and was happy to hear that the town shot them off over the lake. I would have a ring side seat to view them. Wishing him a good day, I headed towards the town to see what stores were there and to get acquainted with everything. As I started walking, my mind went back to Damien. I couldn't think about him without a wave of desire coming over me. What is wrong with me? Those lips on mine, those fingers in me, I have to get a grip on my emotions. It was a one shot deal. I didn't think he would call me again so I might as well move on from this. I have a job to do when I'm here and I plan on doing it well. I don't need any distractions whatsoever anyway. Well, that's what I keep telling myself. Who am I fooling?

Taking the list out of my bag, I saw a few stores

that I could purchase what I needed. Running in and out of the stores, I purchased linens, decorative pillows for the couch, some pots and pans for the kitchen too. I was able to have them delivered to the apartment which saved me from lugging everything back in this heat. Once that was all done, I saw a women's clothing boutique on the corner. Now, that's just what I need. I loved the window displays and saw that the fashions were current. I decided to go and see what they have. Opening the door, a bell tingled overhead.

"Hello there, welcome to my store."

"Thank you very much." Seeing a dress that caught my eye, I headed right to the rack to look at it.

"Now that would be absolutely lovely on you with your coloring, so festive too."

It was a gorgeous deep magenta color, form fitting and slightly off the shoulder. I agreed with the saleswoman, the color would look great with my exotic coloring. And they had my size 4 too. Grabbing it off the rack, I headed in the back to the dressing room.

"I can't wait to see it on you love. My name is Maddie, are you new in town?"

"Yes, I am. I start working this week over at Stone Oil Industries and just moved here from New Jersey. I'm Selina Harrison."

"Well welcome Selina Harrison. Would you love something to drink? Ice tea, some wine?"

"Ice tea would be great. So what do you think?"

I stepped out of the dressing room and loved this dress. It clung to my curves where it should. For a size 4, I have a somewhat hourglass figure, this dress made me feel so sexy and classy. I just hope I would have someplace and someone to wear it for.

"Wow Selina, you are gorgeous in it! I hate you; I could never wear something like this."

I also needed some undergarments and saw that Maddie had quite a collection.

"I'll take this dress and some of the lingerie too. I have a feeling this is going to become my favorite store."

"Oh I hope so. I think we are going to become friends too." Maddie had a fun personality and just a genuine person. I instantly felt at ease with her. It would be nice to have a friend here as Julia was so far away. So putting the 3 bra and panty sets on the counter, the magenta dress, I also found a pair of white linen pants with a pastel blue linen top that I added to the pile and a sexy nightgown. I don't know why I wanted that, maybe to feel that I'm moving on; maybe Damien brought that out of me. Who knows? Paying for everything, I sat at a chair by her counter and sipped my tea.

"So tell me about yourself Selina. So why all the way cross country for work?"

I felt that I could talk to her so I spilled it out to her, my breakup, right down to meeting Damien but not what happened on the flight. I really was coming to terms with what happened on the flight anyway but it was our time, our memories.

"I have to commend you for doing what you needed to do for yourself. It's a blessing in disguise to find out about the ex before you were married. What a mess that would have been after the fact!"

"That's what I keep telling myself when I get a down about it. I just can't believe he did that to me."

"Here's to moving on." Maddie clinked her glass to mine on that toast.

"Now you are a Geologist. That must be very interesting work."

"Yes it is. Everything that we do to our earth, especially with off shore drilling and fracking, has an impact on our lives. I'm here to guide Mr. Stone and his company in making the right decisions for our environment."

"I'm sure you will do a great job at the company. Hey I just thought of this. Do you have any plans for this afternoon? My friends are having a BBQ at the park; I would love to have you join us. It's very casual, they are businessmen and women; some own local businesses in town and some even work over at Stone. It would be great to have you come on by for it."

"You know, that would be really nice, I just have plans on doing the rest of the unpacking but that can wait until tomorrow. What can I bring?"

"Just a bottle of wine, how's that? We have all of the food ordered, we just show up at the park. It's right over there down at the hill. If you want, I'm closing my shop at three today, why don't you meet me here and then we can go over there together. I hate when I go to a new place and don't know anyone. I will be there to introduce you to everyone."

"That sounds great. Thank you for everything and for the talk. I appreciate it. Here's my number so you have it." We exchanged cell numbers and then taking my packages, I told her I would see her later.

I really liked Maddie and knew I would become friends with her as time went on. Now I just needed to find a liquor store and purchase a few bottles of wine. This is going to be a nice afternoon. I would get to meet quite a few people and even some from Stone Oil. Finding a liquor store on my way back to my condo, I picked up a few bottles of wine. Deciding to add a few for myself, I took my time walking back to the condo. Damien crossed my mind again and that had to stop. Unless he calls me, there isn't anything there for me.

Chapter 10 Damien's afternoon

Happy July 4th weekend to me. Getting out of the shower, I had a little bit of time before I headed over to Steve's for their annual family BBQ. I knew I would be drilled by his mom about my current love life now that I moved on from my former girlfriend Lauren Saylor. She just got to be too much for me, clingy, was pushing to get married. Unfortunately, she wasn't taking the breakup well and still tries to be a part of my life. I'm not one to be cruel to another person but it's getting to the point that she is putting us in a position for me to take that route. She just wasn't who I saw myself ending up with happily forever after. Now Selina was a different story. But who knows what is going to happen when I walk into our staff meeting after the holiday. I haven't text her as there wasn't anything to say as CEO. Unless she texts me with a question, there was no reason for me to reach out to her.

This is going to be the longest two days of my life. Heading down to the garage, I got into my Corvette. During the week, DT drives me but I love driving and enjoy a drive to unwind after a crazy week. The thought of having Selina next to me with the top down, well, just thinking about her has me wanting her. As I pulled up to the liquor store, I saw a woman walking down the street that looked like Selina. As I looked closely, I realized it is her. I stay in my car, just looking at her carrying a few packages back towards the condo. She has incredible legs and such a gorgeous ass. Unfortunately, I can't let her see me. I would love nothing more than to take her with me to the party but I can't let her know who I am until we go to work. Putting my head back against the seat, I got myself under control and finally went into the liquor store for a few cases of Corona.

Loading up the Corvette, I pulled out of the space and head on over to Steve's house. I can't stop thinking about how Selina responded to my touch. She came alive when I touched her. Thinking of her lips crushed under mine and hearing her cries made me want her even more, all of her. Reaching between my legs to adjust myself, I pull into Steve's driveway. His kids playing basketball in the driveway, I decided to back the car out and park it on the street.

"Sorry Uncle Damien. We promise not to hit your car." Grabbing the cases of beer, I head on over to see them. Steve's kids were good young men, they were very respectful but I wasn't going to be a fool to park the Corvette in the driveway.

"Hey guys, how are you? Where's your Dad?"

"He's in the back at the grill. Do you need help?"

"No, I'm good. See you guys later."

So I headed around back to meet up with everyone. Putting the beer by the coolers, I grab two of them and walk over to Steve at the BBQ.

"Hey buddy, how are you doing?"

"Hey Damien. Steer clear of my mom; she is looking for you now that you are single again. She swears she has someone that you have to meet. I already told her to leave you alone but I think between your mom and my mom, they pledged together they will get you married off."

"Thanks for the warning but I just may have things under control myself." Taking a swig out of my Corona, I saw Steve raise his eyebrows high into his forehead.

"Well that's some news D. Who is she?"

"You wouldn't believe me if I told you."

"Try me."

"Without getting into everything, I met her on the flight to Houston last night. Turns out to be our new Geologist. The thing is I didn't tell her who I was. The rest of it is between Selina and me."

"Jesus Damien. You are playing with fire here but then again, that's you. Wow, I gotta hand it to you. You don't do anything on a small scale. Can't wait until the fireworks at the staff meeting when we get back."

"Yeah but she is so worth the wrath I'll face at the office. I'm sure it's nothing that I can't handle, in fact, I'm looking forward to the challenge."

"Well, I'll back you up my friend, especially if things start flying in the office. So is she worth the fight?"

"Yep, definitely." I started smiling when I thought of Selina. She was definitely worth the fight.

"Ok, I'll tell my mom that you are working on someone and that she needs to back off. Here, have a burger. So besides the attraction you have towards her, how is she as a Geologist? Good idea to have her on board with us?"

"Yes, absolutely. She is one of the best in her field. She was going to teach, that's why she turned down this job initially. Her fiancée didn't work out and Selina reached out to me as asked if the job was still available."

"A fiancée? I hope that you won't be a rebound relationship for her."

" I don't plan on being a rebound anything Steve. You know me better than that."

"No I can't imagine you would ever put yourself in that position. It's either all or nothing for you. Now with Lauren, she isn't taking no for an answer. She happened to call my wife today to find out if you were going to be here. Denise told her no, you weren't going to make it."

"Remind me to kiss your wife for that lie. I don't know what to do with Lauren. I'm getting to the point that I'm going to really end up hurting her. How about telling your mom to help find her another guy?"

"Hey now, that's an idea! I will just go ahead and do that." And so the rest of the afternoon was very nice. I enjoyed seeing my staff that was there: I made sure that I was just a friend and not their boss. I didn't want anyone to feel uncomfortable. I visited with Steve's mom for a bit too. She wasn't too bad with her advice in finding a woman. Steve already told her to leave me alone as I did meet someone and was working on her. Looking at the time, I really needed to get going. I had some paperwork to do for the meeting on Tuesday. Thanking Steve and Denise for a great afternoon, I jumped into my car and headed back into the city to my condo.

Chapter 11 Selina's afternoon

The people that I met this afternoon couldn't be nicer to me. I was able to meet a few of the other employees from Stone and we had a great conversation on the upcoming drilling and my take on it. This was my specialty. I love when I can get people's attention on what drilling does to our environment even though I do recognize the importance of our oil dependency in this country. I'm even hoping to change the CEO's thoughts to clean energy. Why not? I could definitely try. I know I have to get my report together tomorrow for my presentation to the board and the CEO on Tuesday. I already had my outline, just had to put my power point presentation together. I plan on making a good argument on this drilling site but will think about it tomorrow and not at the picnic. I met the CFO Thomas Hutchings and his wife Theresa, and a few of the drillers who were very interested in what my take was on their current plan. I told them my report was going to be presented to the Board on Tuesday with my recommendations. I also met my new assistant Mike. I didn't even think I would have someone working with me so it was a pleasant surprise to meet him. He had his business degree but started taking science classes in the evening to become more familiar with the work he would be doing with me. I was very impressed with this and just clicked with him. I was introduced to his partner Chris and really liked them on the spot. I couldn't thank Maddie enough for introducing me to her friends and felt welcome in a strange city. Seeing that it was getting late, I thanked all of them and needed to head on home. Mike and Chris were heading out too so they gave me a lift to the complex to see me safely home.

"Thanks for the lift. I'll see you on Tuesday and look forward to working with you Mike."

"Thanks Selina. I'm looking forward to it too."

As they drove off, I knew I wanted to get moving on that report for Tuesday. Actually I was looking forward to it but wanted to Skype with Julie first. I knew this conversation would be girly talk as I needed her advice so grabbing a glass of wine, I fired up my laptop and got a connection to her. I got myself comfortable in the couch that hugged me and waited for her to connect in with me.

Well hello Ms. Texas. How are you doing? You have some color already.

Hey there yourself. I was invited to a picnic today so I went and met some nice people; a few from the job too. They were curious about my presentation on Tuesday.

You are going to knock it out of the park at that meeting. I know how passionate you are about drilling and the environment. I wish I were there to see you in action.

Thanks Jules. Well, I'm calling about something else. Actually, I met someone on the flight here and well, let's just say things got out of hand on the flight over.

You have got to be kidding me? You finally have a one night stand in the mile high club after this past month of me telling you to just go for it? Wow Sel. How was he?

I can't talk about this but it was amazing for what we could actually do in our seats. On top of that, he was gorgeous and very kind. I lost it when the flight took off, everything started crashing down on me that I should have been on my honeymoon and cancelling the wedding, seeing the ex with his nurse. The few drinks I had in me made me lose it. He placed his hanky in my hand and then held my hand until I could get myself together. I ended up having another drink and told him everything and well, things just happened.

The good thing about Skype is that you can see the others reaction during a conversation like this.

I like him already. Hold this thought. I'll be right back.

Julia left the screen and came back in a few moments with a glass and a bottle of wine. Laughing at her, she poured a nice amount, took a big gulp and just started laughing.

You did what people read about in the hot romance novels Sel. I'm shocked but happy for you. What happened when you landed?

I gave him my card with my cell number on it and we went our separate ways. With my luck, he is probably married. I can't imagine I would hear from him again. I'm hoping but thinking maybe not. I haven't heard from him yet

You never know Sel. But I'm happy you went out of your comfort zone. Good for you. Who says women can't get the same pleasures as men, even opportunities and spur of the moment hot sex? He might have thought you used him too.

I think I tried to give him that impression but there was something in his eyes that let me know we weren't done yet.

Ooh, I love that Sel. Handsome?

Yes, and then some. Dark hair, blue eyes, beard, body of living death and a tattoo that goes from his forearm to God knows where. You know how I love tattoos on a man. I wonder if he has others. Something tells me he does. I'm guessing late 30's.

Yep, you're a goner. Let's toast to a possible future with this hottie. And if not him, maybe you'll have an affair with your CEO. You never know.

Laughing at Julie, we touched our glasses to the screen and decided it was time to sign off.

I have to get my report all set for Tuesday. I'll keep

*you posted on what happens on Tuesday and
Skype with you then.*

Sure Sel. Good luck and Happy 4th.

As I saw Julia's image disappear from the screen, I
thanked my lucky stars that I had such a dear
friend to confide in. Something told me that I'm
going to need her next week.

Grabbing my yoga wear, I jumped in the shower to
get myself ready to work late in the evening. I
thought of how the presentation would go, how I
would dress and the points I definitely wanted to
make. That's what the CEO hired me to do and I
plan on educating all of them in that room on
Tuesday morning.

As I toweled dried my hair, I thought that I should
reach out to Mr. Stone to see how much time he
would allot me to speak. That would be important
to the content of my report. So grabbing my cell
phone, I put in a text to him.

*Mr. Stone, Sorry to bother you on the holiday
weekend. I'm working on my presentation to the*

Board and just needed to know how much time you are allocating me for my findings/report?

I didn't have long to wait for his answer. I was surprised by this as I thought that maybe with the holiday weekend, he might be away with family.

Dr. Harrison, I'm happy to see that you are hard at work on this report but I hope that you are also enjoying some time this holiday weekend. How about 30 minutes? I know the Board is very interested in what you have to say.

Mr. Stone, 30 minutes is just perfect. I certainly don't want to bore anyone but make the maximum explanations with the presentation; the pros and cons of this drilling site. I'm guessing I would have access to power point?

Good Dr. I leave all of this in your very capable hands and look forward to hearing what your findings are. And yes, you will have access to power point. I hope that you also had a nice time today and were able to get out.

Yes Sir. I met some new friends and was invited to a BBQ at the park nearby. I met my assistant Mike and your CFO and his wife too. It was a beautiful day. I wish you a good night. If I have any other questions, I'll be sure to reach out to you. Until then, I look forward to meeting you on Tuesday.

Good night Dr.

Well, that went well. I have 30 minutes to make my case, charm them, let them know that I have a brain in my head for this work and see what I can do to make sure I will be a good asset to the team. I've already started winning over the drillers as they really didn't see why the boss would bring in a Geologist but now they get it. I really am excited that I made the right choice in coming to Houston. Staying in New Jersey was going to bury me. Grabbing a bottle of water and putting the radio on for some background noise, I opened my laptop to start putting my presentation together. I plan on making this a long night.

Chapter 12 Damien

So I'm sitting at my desk, doing the outline for my presentation to the board when a message came thru to my phone. It's from Selina. Well, I have to admit my heart did miss a beat when I saw it was her even though I know it's a question about work. Seeing that she wanted to know how long her presentation could be and if she had access to power point, well that was easy to answer. To see that she was at a BBQ and met my CFO as well as her new assistant, I prayed that nothing else was said about me that she could connect the dots. I didn't take her to be anything but an intelligent person that just one slip from someone and I would be finished before even starting with her. As I continued to answer the text, I knew I was in the clear. Running my hand thru my hair, I realized that this was a pretty shitty thing to have done to her but if things work out as planned, what a story to tell our kids, when they grew up that is. Realizing how late it was, I saw that she was a workaholic like me. Another good thing in the right column. Lauren was anything but that. She wanted to be pampered and often. That got tired and quickly. But now I'm doing exactly what Selina might be doing. She might be comparing me to her fiancée and I'm comparing her to Lauren. That stops now. There is no comparison. Selina was the type of woman that I might have been searching for but we'll see after her presentation on Tuesday. If I have to strong arm her as her boss, so be it. I'm not going down without a fight. I've already had a taste of her and definitely wasn't done with her. Oh Hell, I'm not getting this report done now. Slamming the laptop cover down, I grabbed the remote and turned on the TV for something mindless to watch. Sleep was evading me; really, I'm a mess just thinking about her. Ok, a glass of scotch. That would help knock me out. Tomorrow is the picnic with my family and then Tuesday is here.

Chapter 13 Finished

Happy July 4th to me! My report is all complete; the power point is all set. I'm so happy with how this report has come out. I can't wait to start my new job. I feel energized just thinking about it. It's three am and my body is starting to drag. Tomorrow is a day to finish unpacking and just relax before my big day at Stone Industries. The only thing missing is hearing from Damien. Who am I kidding that I could do a one night stand? That's not me. When I think about how he took charge of us, how he sort of dominated me and how he made me feel, I just wanted more of him. But it's impossible as I don't know how to find him. Hitting my pillow in frustration, I hug it to myself and just resign myself to the fact that he could have been an amazing lover. I enjoyed the time we had together and am grateful for having that experience.

Chapter 14 Damien's Parents

"Hey Mom. Hey Dad. Where are you guys?" "In the back son." I heard my Mom answer me so I walked towards their backyard where my parents are with my brother Richard, my sister Dawn and their spouses and kids. Seeing the kids throwing water balloons at my Dad and having him run around the tree to protect himself from the onslaught was a great sight to behold. Gone was the tough CEO when he ran the company to a good family man and Grandpa. Hugging my sister and brother, I was the oldest of the three of us. Of course, I never hear the end of it that I'm not married and that I haven't provided my parents with grandkids. I love them dearly but they need to just relax about it. It's something that I brace myself for whenever we get together. Hopefully Steve's mom told my mom I might have someone in the wings.

"There's my son, Happy July 4th Damien. You are looking well."

"Thanks Mom. Happy 4th everyone. How are you guys doing?"

My sister was the first to answer.

"Well, the kids are driving me insane with school being out. They are both crazy and on my last nerve. I can't wait until they go to camp tomorrow. I'm glad they are going after Dad right now; we were all targeted before you got here. I threatened not to give them any ice cream if they pounded us with the balloons. It seemed to have worked for a little bit."

My sister loved her kids desperately but didn't

have any tolerance for their antics. Having two boys within two years of each other would have tried my patience too. Now my brother Richard has a boy and a girl. His wife declared the "factory" closed as they have one of each.

"The firm is going well D. I'm happy with the clientele we have and the accountants on staff. The kids are great; they head to camp tomorrow with Dawn's kids so we will all have some peace and quiet around the house. How about you?"

"Well, our new Geologist starts tomorrow with her presentation to the Board. It's the start of a new era in this business that we are excited about. Other than that, it's business as usual."

My sister was never one to mince words and came right out with it.

"Aren't you forgetting one thing D? Mom mentioned that you might have a new girl in your life now that you got rid of Lauren."

"I hope to have her in my life. Too soon to tell Dawn. Can we give this a rest? And thanks Mom for telling them. I'll let you all know if something happens."

"You have a new girl in your life son? Your Mother

and I are so happy that you got rid of Lauren. She wasn't right for you. You need the female version of you."

"Thanks Dad. I'll keep you all posted on my love life. What's for lunch Mom? I can't stay late as I have the presentation to finish up tonight."

"Your Father kind of figured you would have to leave early so everything is ready now. Let's go enjoy."

So I got through the rest of the picnic, had a nice time with my niece and nephews and headed out to get started on my report. I found my Dad walking me out to the car and knew he wanted to speak to me about work.

"Son, I just want you to know how proud I am of what you have done with our company. I'll be there tomorrow in the capacity of a Board Member and also with curiosity in meeting Dr. Harrison. I'm hoping she will be the answer to the latest problems we've been having on site. I know there is something we are missing here."

"I'm sure she will Dad. So I'll see you tomorrow at 10, ok? Have a great night."

Pulling away from their house, I breathed a sigh of

relief that I got thru the interrogation. I love my family dearly but like anyone else, they can be a pain in the ass. Smiling at the thought that my sister was the one to jump into the line of questioning with Mom just sitting looking so innocent, well, they definitely knew how to tag team me. Driving into the complex, I headed upstairs to my condo. I made a decision that I was going to text Selina. I knew that I shouldn't but my over anxious self couldn't help it. I needed to have some contact with her. Grabbing my personal cell phone so the number was different, I reached out to her.

Hi Selina. It's me, Damien. How are you?

Her answer seemed to take forever as I just stared at the screen.

Hi Damien. Happy July 4th to you. How are you?

I'm well. Hope you had a great day. Did you do anything special?

No, I finished the report early this am I have to give at work tomorrow. I just finished unpacking and planning on watching the fireworks from my deck tonight. You?

I was at my parents today for their annual BBQ with my sister and brother and their brood. I have work to do today too so I cut my visit short. The reason why I'm writing is to let you know that I have been thinking about you and if you wanted to get together for dinner on Wednesday night?

Selina didn't answer right away which had me a bit worried.

I have to ask you this and please don't think this is an odd question. Are you married?

No, absolutely not. My parents wish that everyday but no. LOL. I haven't met the right woman yet.

Ok, Wednesday is good Damien. Let me get thru my first day tomorrow and we can touch base.

Let's say 7pm and I'll pick you up. You can text me your address tomorrow when you know if that time is good for you. Have a good night Princess.

You too Damien. Thank you for reaching out to me.

Well, ok then. Oh she is going to be pissed tomorrow.

Chapter 15 The Text

Oh my God, Damien sent me a text! Things are looking up for me. New job, new home, maybe a new guy. And he says he's not married. Just my luck. Ok, I'll take things one day at a time. I can't help but have a goofy smile on my face at the thought of seeing him again. I'll wear the new magenta dress I bought at Maddie's. Nothing would make me feel wonderful and feminine but wearing that outfit. I'll pair it with the beautiful black lingerie set I purchased too, just in case. Now it's almost time for fireworks. Grabbing a glass of wine, I have a ringside seat to wish America a very Happy Birthday. As the first fireworks explode in the sky, the inner child in me just looks at them with amazement. I see my neighbor's also sitting on their decks and wave to them. There would be plenty of time to get to know them. Right now, I just want to enjoy and live in the moment that Damien text me. Almost as soon as they started the fireworks, it seemed the Grand Finale started. They were pretty good, not as good as the ones in New York but not too bad overall. I locked up the deck sliding door and headed back to my bedroom to make sure my navy dress was all pressed for the morning. It was one of my favorite dresses, not too formal but not too sexy either. It was perfect for my presentation with sexy navy pumps. I would look presentable but not like a science nerd to the Board. First impressions were everything and I plan on making a good first impression. Reaching my new romance novel, I decided I could get a few chapters in before falling asleep. Saying a prayer of thanks, I realized I was more tired than I thought. Well, so much for reading. I turned off the light and got a good night's sleep.

Chapter 16 The Presentation

I can't look any better than this. Looking into the mirror, my navy dress hugged my curves, dipped into a little "V" in the front and also in the back. Since my legs were tan, I did away with any type of stockings in this heat. My navy pumps showed them off to their best advantage. I had my hair down in waves and pulled it into a low pony tail with wisps of hair framing my face. My makeup was subtle but enhanced my exotic look. I wanted the Board to take me seriously but I didn't want to look unpolished. Packing my laptop, I ran into the kitchen for a quick snack and some coffee. I saw that I had twenty minutes before DT picked me up so I had my breakfast and did some breathing exercises to calm my nerves a bit.

I knew I had this. I just wanted to make my points, be taken seriously and do my job. That's all I could ask for. Seeing it was time to head downstairs to meet DT, I made sure I had my apartment key card as well as my key card for the office, my laptop and handbag.

Knowing he would be prompt, DT was standing

outside the passenger door waiting for me.

"Good morning Selina. Ready for today?"

"Yes DT. Thank you for picking me up."

"No problem, let's get you to work."

So I settled into the back seat and smoothed down my dress. I was a bit nervous as I should be. This was totally normal. I just kept telling myself I was one of the best Geologists in my field, well respected and published. I can handle a CEO and his Board of Directors. Pulling up to the curb, I let myself out of the car just as DT came running over to my side.

"Please don't feel you have to hold the door for me DT. It's totally not necessary."

"You are just like the Boss. He hates when I do that too. Good luck today Selina even though I'm sure you won't need it."

I gave him a wink and walked into my new life at Stone Oil Industries. The lobby was very impressive and immense. Walking to security, I showed them my badge and key card. Welcoming me to the company, they pointed to the rear bank elevators to take me to the Executive offices. Seems I would be on the main floor with the CEO,

CFO, VP and the Board. Now this was both impressive and unexpected. Getting off on the 25th floor, I walked over to the main check in desk and introduced myself. A woman and a man manned the front desk. Lisa and William handled all of the clients coming to see any of us on this floor. Lisa took me to my new office down the hall from the CEO. She explained that Mr. Stone was in a meeting with his assistant and would see me at the staff meeting at ten o'clock. Everyone was expected to convene in the main conference room by nine forty-five as Mr. Stone was very prompt and would start the meeting right on time. She showed me to the corner office which was right next to the CFO and VP. I was very impressed by this as I didn't think I would rank near these officers. Lisa pointed out where Mike sat. Thanking her for everything, I signaled Mike to meet me in my office as I wanted to discuss the power point presentation with him since I wanted him with me in the meeting.

"Good morning Selina. Welcome. I just want to say how excited I am to work with you."

"I'm glad you feel that way as I'm going to have

you handle my power point presentation for me this morning. Are you ok with that?"

"Yes absolutely."

"Great, grab your coffee and show me where to get mine as we have a presentation to run thru quickly before the meeting."

"It's down the hall to the left. I'll be right back to get this set up with you."

I quickly put my laptop on my desk and other printed materials. Heading out to the kitchen, I passed Thomas's office. I waved to him as I made my way down the hall.

"Selina. Hey, how are you doing?"

"I'm headed over for coffee before I go thru my power point presentation with Mike."

"I won't keep you as the Boss doesn't like to be kept waiting. I'll talk to you later. Good luck."

"Thanks Tom."

As I passed the Vice-President's office, I noticed that he just stared at me for a few seconds before waving to me. I figured I would have time to meet everyone after the meeting. I would feel better getting Mike up to speed before I spent time saying hello. Reaching for a cup, another hand followed mine to the cabinet. Looking over to the person standing next to me, I saw it was the VP that I just passed by.

"Excuse me, are you Dr. Harrison?"

"Yes, please call me Selina."

"Steve Miller, VP of the firm. It's very nice to meet you." After he shook my hand, he told me he would see me later at the meeting, grabbed his coffee and headed back to his office.

Walking quickly back to my office, I saw that Mike was there and already had my laptop set up for me. I could tell now he was going to be a life saver. Going thru the entire presentation quickly, he told me not to worry. He would take cues from me and he would move the presentation at my pace. He found out how many officers would be attending and made sure enough copies were printed out and all collated for me. I couldn't thank him enough. I had a half hour before Mike came to get me for the meeting. Standing at the window, I just stood there as I surveyed downtown Houston. As I looked out over the water I saw where the drilling sites were. I planned on getting out there this week, maybe even tomorrow. I would do my ground work in the office first. Within a few days, my life was definitely looking up. I have already felt good at my job and knew I could make a difference. I just can't get Damien out of my mind; what that man did to me in such a short time. I can't believe how those lips and hands made me feel as they explored my body; and that tattoo. Seriously Selina, time to get a grip on things. I've never felt this way before with anyone.

Hearing a knock at my door, I saw Mike standing there indicating that it was time to go to the conference room. He told me the usual set up would be him sitting behind me against the wall. When it was my time for the presentation, I would move to the front of the room and he would move to my chair to operate the power point. He had a bottle of water for me too.

"What would I do without you Mike?"

"You will do well Selina and you look amazing too." Giving him a playful nudge, we both headed down to the main conference room. As we walked in, heads turned our way. Mike went to his area to set up the power point. I nodded to the various members and saw Thomas again. As he shook my hand, he introduced me to Mr. Stone Senior.

"Mr. Stone, it's an honor to meet you Sir."

"Nice to meet you too Dr. Harrison. Your reputation precedes you. My son has told me wonderful things about you. He has faith that you will help bring this company to new heights."

"I hope so Sir. I'm going to do my very best." Mr. Stone moved over to the section where the other Board members were sitting down. I noticed several were looking me with admiration and some with skepticism. It was my job to win them over today and I would do my very best. It was ten o'clock and the doors opened to Mr. Damien Stone.

"Please take your seats."

As I turned around at the sound of his voice, the floor could have opened and swallowed me up. What the Hell? The man of my dreams was standing in from of the room. The man that I opened myself up to in more ways than one was my Boss!

Steve noticed that I was just standing there with my mouth open and grabbed me by the waist. He whispered in my ear as he guided me to my seat. "Please give him a chance to explain when the meeting is over. You have a job to do right now. He is counting on you."

"You are kidding me, right?" Sitting down in my seat, I couldn't even look at Damien. This is an absolute nightmare. And he knew! How the Hell did he know who I was on the flight? And not tell me who he was? Oh my God, I didn't ask for his full name. Now who was the fool? Everything came crashing down on me. The crying, telling him my story, what went on under the blankets. Oh my God. What I did under the blankets! He's my Boss! I think within a minute, I went through every emotion; from being shocked to humiliated to being extremely pissed off.

"Good morning everyone. Welcome to our quarterly business meeting. I thank the Board for being present here, including my Father as we go thru the earnings as well as introduce our new employee, Dr. Selina Harrison."

A round of applause went around the room. I just stared at Damien and coolly nodded my head at him. His eyes bored right into me, almost daring me to let everyone know our secret. Turning my face from his, I acknowledged everyone else around the room. Keeping my face down at my paperwork, I worked to recover my composure before I had to give my presentation. Mike tapped me on the shoulder to hand me the bottle of water. Steve looked at me with a worried look on his face. I was pissed. First the asshole and now someone that I felt a connection with, betrayed my trust and took advantage of who I was. Damien even text me last night, asking me for dinner on Wednesday. That's it. I'm done before we have started. I can't do this with him.

"And now, I would love to turn our program over to Dr. Selina Harrison." Hearing Damien announce my name, I shook myself out of my murderous thoughts.

Grabbing my own folder and one for Damien, I walked up to the room as calm as collected as I could be. Damien waited for me at the podium and extended his hand to shake mine. As soon as we touched hands, the shock of his touch brought me back to our flight just three days ago. I let go of his hand quickly and handed him the paperwork. On the outside, I presented the professional woman I was, but on the inside, I fought down my emotions of what we shared together. Stepping up to the microphone, I started my lecture.

"Good morning. I would like to thank Mr. Stone for giving me this opportunity to work with Stone Oil Industries and to be a part of this wonderful company. Let me start by explaining what I'm being hired to do, especially for the Board members so they know where their money is being spent. (I heard a few chuckles around the room at that comment.) Mr. Stone is working to bring this company to the next level, to be more aware of how drilling and fracking are detrimental to the Earth's environment. Everything that we do to our Earth's crust can have serious repercussions. While I know that profits are a huge margin for any company, being environmentally sound is a major step in the right direction to keeping this world safe for future generations as well as being energy dependent from other countries, including the Middle East. I have a power point presentation all set up to explain in detail what I have researched and discovered in your drilling sites off the Texas coastline where you are having some setbacks I can only give you my recommendations. You will have the final say. So let's begin."

As Mike worked thru the presentation with me, I glanced over at Damien to make my point and I can only say the look on his face was one of admiration. I shine when I talk about Geology and if I can get my ideas into other people's minds to change their way of thinking, then I have done my job. I explained to the Board that the reason they are having a problem with this drilling site was that it sat near a fault line. Moving the drilling over in either direction would help to stabilize the area. "And that concludes my presentation. Do you have any questions?"

"Yes Dr. Harrison. My name is Winston Clooney, one of the members of the Board. Any chance your Father is Dr. Sean Harrison?"

"Yes Sir. Dr. Harrison is my Father. He is a Paleontologist. He gave me my love of science. Why do you ask?"

"He's more than just a Paleontologist; he has

made incredible discoveries in his career. Well, I went to college with him, I won't say how long ago that was but now my son works with him at NYU. He wants to follow in his footsteps. Do you mind if I ask you where you did your studies?"

"I did my undergraduate work at Columbia and my Master's and Doctorate at NYU. I have traveled around the world to study fault lines in various countries, including our own in LA and New York. In regards to oil research, my studies include the Middle East, particularly Kuwait and Saudi Arabia. My Father has been a tremendous influence in the line of work I do. He handles discoveries of species from thousands of years ago while I work with the world that we inhabit to help protect it for future generations."

I noticed that Mr. Stone "Senior" had everyone's attention next as he addressed me.

"Dr. Harrison, at first I told my son I wasn't sold on bringing on a Geologist to advise us but I can see now that we can only benefit from your knowledge. Thank you for your candor and for your research. We look forward to hearing more from you as your time with us continues."

"Thank you Mr. Stone." I walked off the podium without a second glance at Damien. I was just disgusted and upset with myself too; it wasn't just Damien's fault.

Shaking Mike's hand, he went back to his own seat as I sat back down between Tom and Steve.

"That was incredible Doctor." Steve squeezed my arm and gave me a smile.

"Now, we will take a twenty minute break. See you back here by 11:30."

As everyone including myself got up, I heard Damien say to me, "Not you Dr. Harrison. A moment please."

Steve leaned over to me as he was getting ready to leave.

"Remember what I told you Selina. Please give him a chance to explain." Steve winked at me as he left the room and nodded at Damien. The room cleared out fast. Damien stood facing me until he took off his jacket. As he sat on the corner of the desk, he loosened his tie and unbuttoned a few buttons. His eyes never left mine.

"First of all, your presentation was flawless. I noticed that you turned quite a few of the stubborn minds around with your explanations and I thank you for that. You will definitely be a great asset to this company."

I didn't even acknowledge his compliment and definitely didn't blink an eye. If I could throw something at him, I would have. As he looked right into my eyes, Damien definitely had an idea about how angry I was.

"I'm sorry about all of this. If you knew who I was from the beginning, nothing would have happened between us and that wasn't acceptable to me. I felt something, a connection from the beginning with you," explained Damien.

"I opened myself up to you, I did things that I wouldn't have done with anyone, especially my Boss. I can't believe this is happening." I just put my head down for a second.

"Princess."

"Don't you dare call me that! This changes everything." I can't believe the man that occupied my thoughts and dreams has now become my Boss. How can I have a relationship with him? I'm so disappointed about the whole situation and in myself. Oh my God, how I responded to him came crashing down around me. Sensing that Damien was standing in front of me, he grabbed me by the arms.

"I don't regret for one single moment what we shared together. You have been in my thoughts and my desires all weekend. I don't give a damn that we work together, we can get around this. I need to know more about you, all of you Selina. Just give us time. I'm so sorry to make you feel that I betrayed you. I had my own selfish reasons to keep my identity from you. Look at me Selina." Raising my eyes up to his, I saw the stormy blues of his eyes boring into mine.

"I will not lie to you any longer. I want you. I want you so much that it hurts. I want to bury myself deep inside you and make you cry out my name. I want to make you forget your fiancé and be mine in every way possible. And I will not stop until I have you."

Pulling my arm from his, I reached up to slap him in the face but didn't make it. He stopped my hand in mid slap and pulled me up against him. Slamming his mouth on top of mine, his lips devoured me. Biting my lower lip, I opened my mouth as he drove his tongue into mine, twisting and teasing me. It was just like it was on the plane. This man ignited something deep within me. Pulling his mouth from mine, his lips traveled to the pulse beating wildly in my neck. Hearing a moan escape from my lips, I begged him to stop. I knew I had to get my thoughts in order and get away from him before it was too late.

"Please Damien, stop."

Looking at me, I couldn't stop my lip from quivering.

"I'm so sorry to have lifted my hand to you. It will never happen again. And this can't happen again. Not now." Damien stopped and dropped his arms from mine. Walking to his jacket, he picked it up.

"Ok Dr. Harrison. Be ready for dinner tonight at 7 o'clock. It's a business dinner with Tom and Steve. They will be bringing their wives so you will be comfortable with us. I will come around with DT to pick you up. Don't be late."

Frowning at Damien, I saw him shrug back into his suit jacket and straighten his tie.

"That is all."

Feeling definitely dismissed, I gathered my things

and exited the conference room to the safety of my office.

Chapter 17 The Fallout

"Hey, is it safe to come in?" Steve stuck his head in the conference room. "Looks like everything's in place in here and you aren't sporting a black eye." He couldn't help but chuckle.
"It doesn't mean that she didn't try. She did apologize for trying to hit me but I caught her and then kissed the Hell out of her. Where this woman is concerned, I have no boundaries or control."
"Well that is attraction and love my friend. How did you end it?"
"Selina begged me to stop and I dismissed her. Pulled the "Boss" act like I knew I would have to. I told her to be ready by 7 o'clock tonight with you, Tom, and your wives. Then I told her she was dismissed." I stood by the window and ran my hand thru my hair. If it's at all possible, my attraction to her was even greater than it was three days ago.
"Ok my friend. At least Selina knows now. Give

her time to process everything and we'll try to smooth things over tonight. I hope you don't mind by I told Denise about this. Maybe she can help from a woman's point of view."

"That's fine Steve. Can't be any worse than what it is now."

"I wouldn't count on that. Denise can't believe you did this and was quite vocal in her objections about it. I'll have her calmed down by the time you pick us up but I'm sure she will say something to you."

"No doubt. At least the worst part is over and now I have to work on winning Selina back."

Hearing the door opening, the Board and my senior staff started coming back in the room. Selina wasn't needed for this part of the meeting so her chair was vacant. Wrapping my head around what I needed to do now, I started this meeting and got thru it before lunchtime.

Now with Selina...

Standing by the window, I touched my fingers to my lips, still feeling where he touched me. In an instant, my world tilted on its own axis. The man of my dreams is my Boss. Wow. And He knew the whole time. I was going thru my mind everything that happened on the plane. Damn, right down to DT. He knows too. Damien had this all planned out.

Hearing a knock on my door, I saw Mike smiling at me.

"Come in Mike. Thank you so much for your assistance this morning."

"Selina, you were brilliant. I learned so much from listening to you. I got more out of this than when my professor teaches his lesson."

"I'm sure your professor is just fine but thank you. I'm glad it's over and now I can get down to work. By the way, where can I get something to eat for lunch?"

"Right on the fifth floor. There is a restaurant and also a deli. Take your pick."

"Ok, I'll head out in an hour." As Mike headed back to his desk, I had ocean floor charts to go thru. I wanted to get out to the drill site tomorrow so mapping this out now would be a smart thing to do.

Picking up my Iphone, I sent a quick text to Julie.

Hey Jules. You are not going to believe this. The gorgeous man on the flight that things got a little out of control, well, he turned out to be my BOSS. Yes, that's right, Damien is Damien Stone, CEO and owner of this firm. I just found out right before I had to give my report. He knew the whole time who I was. He apologized right after the meeting and just before I tried to hit him in the face. OMG. I'm mortified that I tried to hit him and what happened on the flight. Now I've been ordered to be ready for dinner tonight with the CFO, VP and their wives.

Hey Sel, Wow. That's insane. He must have his reasons for keeping his identity a secret. He definitely brings out the emotions in you too. I don't ever remember you ever acting like this over a man. Why don't you relax and just go with it?

He did tell me that he isn't giving me up.

Listen Sel. Give him a chance. It's understandable that you are upset and felt that you were lied to.

It's kind of romantic that he would go thru such lengths to be with you but Yes, that doesn't excuse how he did it. So why don't you have fun with this. Torture him a bit, that is if you want to pursue a relationship with him. Make him earn you.

I don't know if I can do that.

Sel, you are gorgeous without trying. Look what he has done so far to be with you. Have some fun with it.

Ok, I'll think about it Jules. I'll let you know what happens.

Listen, you're attracted to him, right?

Yes, I can't stop thinking about him.

So, what's a little fun? Sounds like he is into you. Make him earn you and it! I can't wait to hear more as time goes on. I live such a boring life in Jersey. Keep me posted Sel, ok?

I will Jules. Thank you for always being there. Love you.

Love you too Sel.

Make him earn it. Hmmm. Just might work but first I have to decide what I want from this possible relationship. Right now, I have to get to mapping out the site. I put Damien in the back of my mind and just focused on the work at hand.

Before I knew it, an hour had gone by. My stomach let me know that it was lunchtime, so grabbing my notes, I figured I can work while I was eating to keep ahead of my work. Making my way to the fifth floor, I walked into the deli area and ordered a salad. With what happened almost two hours ago still had me reeling a bit so something light and quick was perfect.

As I started into my research, I heard Damien's familiar voice coming into the deli. I was happy that I was sitting in a slightly darkened corner as he walked in with a blonde. She looked very friendly with him and he had his hand on her back escorting her in. Some speech he gave me in the board room. He must have several different women at his beck and call. Why wouldn't he? I'm such a fool when it comes to men. I tried not to let this bother me but it did. Oh damn. He is sitting five tables away from me. It would only be a matter of time until he saw me sitting here. Seeing the blonde put her arm thru Damien's, I knew I had to get out of there. I can't stand looking at them together. Gathering up my notes, I stood up a little too quickly that my salad crashed to the floor. Damn it, now this will get people's attention. This was really not my day. As I bent down to pick up the bowl and put the lettuce in it, a familiar masculine hand was helping me.

"Selina, let me help you with this."

"I don't want your help or to keep you from your lunch date."

As Damien held my hand in his, I couldn't help but look up at his face.

"She is not a lunch date." It seemed that for a brief second, it was just us together in that deli. Shaking myself from my dreaming, I pulled my hand from his.

"Well, what have we here? And why are you holding her hand Damien?" Asked the blonde.

"Enough Lauren," growled Damien.

"Who are you?" Asked the blonde.

"I'm Dr. Harrison," replied Selina with a bit of edge to her voice.

"Lauren, go sit back at the table and I'll be right there. This isn't any of your concern."

"Damien baby, you don't have to be this way. I just wanted to meet your friend."

"It's either go sit down or leave. Take your pick." Damien's voice lowered to an octave that I've never heard before as he stared at Lauren. Lifting her head high, she spun on her heels and walked back to their table.

"I'm sorry about Lauren," said Damien.

"She is not my concern. Well, I have this and I won't keep you." Using my napkin to clean up the rest of it, I tossed everything in the trash. One of the workers came over to me with a mop. He assured me that he would take care of the rest of the mess and not to worry about it.

Looking at Damien, I wished him a good lunch.

"Enjoy your lunch Mr. Stone. See you tonight." I felt his eyes staring at me as I walked to the elevators. I had my pride but it had a big crack in it right now.

Chapter 18 Dinner Date: Damien's story

The five of us were in the limo on our way over to Selina's. Looking at my two friends, Tom and Steve, I didn't say a word while gazing at their angry wives, Denise and Theresa.

Running my hands thru my hair, I sat there waiting for the interrogation to begin and I knew it was going to come first from Theresa.

"So Damien, is that a new Armani suit you are wearing? I love the no tie look." Theresa sat there with her arms across her chest.

"Here it comes," muttered Tom under his breath.

"Theresa, just say it. We've known each other a long time."

"Ok, as much as what you did was pretty shitty, I understand why you did it."

Both me and Tom said "You do?" at the same time. It was almost comical.

"Yes, I do. Selina would have never opened up to you the way she did had she known you were her boss and you are in love with her."

"What?"

"Yes Damien, you are feeling a strong connection to her. If it's not love or the beginning of that, then I don't know what it is. I can see that. Denise can see that, don't you Denise?"

"Yes, but you have made a damn good mess of things Damien. You lost her trust. So Theresa and I have thought things thru. If you want to win her back, you are going to have to grovel."

Both me and Steve said at the same time, "Grovel?"

"Yes, plenty of it. You need to win her trust back. That means apologies, kind words, gifts, thoughtful gestures; you have to be on her mind 24/7. Do you understand?"

"It's not going to help when Selina saw you with Lauren today too D," said Steve.

"I thought you got rid of her," said Theresa.

"She showed up today right when I was going to the deli for lunch. Selina was there and saw us. As she got up to leave, Selina dropped her salad on the floor. I got up to help her."

"Did she brush you off?" asked Denise.

"Pretty much."

"You have a bit of work to do Damien. If Selina is even remotely interested in you, you basically have to earn her trust."

"Ok, ladies, I'll be the King of the Grovelers."

"Oh this is going to be something to see," laughed Steve.

"She is worth it guys."

The limo came to a stop right in front of her building. No Selina. DT heard our whole discussion and while he would never interject into the conversation, he always had my best interest at heart and knew exactly what needed to be done.

"Hey Boss, I'll go ring her. Be right back."

Watching DT speak to security, I just sat back in my seat. I'm wondering if she is going to defy me and not show up. DT gave us thumbs up thru the window.

"Don't worry D. It's going to be just fine. We are here to help." Denise tried to reassure me. Oh, that's precious. The ladies are going to help me. I looked at Steve and Tom. The three of us started laughing.

"Oh good, here she is," announced Denise.

As I looked over at the main entrance, I see a flash of magenta and two gorgeous legs in about three inch heels walking over to security. DT held the door open for her and if I wasn't sitting down, I would have fallen down. The magenta dress looks like it was poured on her, form fitting and stunning with her dark hair, olive skin and those topaz colored eyes.

"Hey D, close your mouth. Remember grovel, not drool," smiled Denise.

As I watched Selina walk towards the limo, she smiled up at DT over something he said to her. I have to admit, I was jealous that gorgeous smile wasn't directed at me. I'm losing it big time. I hope by the time the evening was over, she would be on her way to forgiving me. I don't know what I would do if she didn't but pushing that thought aside, I have my ways to win her back. I opened the limo door and got out to meet her. Walking over to her, I offered her my arm which I was glad that she took. Leaning close to her ear, I caught the sexy cologne that lingered on her neck and hair.

"I know I shouldn't say this but you look stunning."

"No you shouldn't." As she stopped on the sidewalk, I motioned DT towards the driver seat.

"Let's make something clear Mr. Stone. You are my boss and I am your employee. What happened a few days ago will not happen again. I would appreciate that we keep this professional so I can do the job that I was hired to do." Moving her arm from mine, she walked the rest of the way to the limo on her own accord. Damned if I didn't want to grab this woman, throw her over my shoulder and basically have my way with her.

Now I know that this wasn't going to be easy but I love a challenge. Selina looked so adorable when she was angry but I let her think that I was agreeable to her demand when I didn't say a word. As she got into the limo, I heard the girls introducing themselves to her as I climbed in right after her. My eyes caught Tom and Steve's in an understanding of my task at hand as the girls wanted to know where Selina bought that dress. Hearing the name of Selina's favorite boutique, I filed that away for future gifts for her. I plan on making this a mission with this groveling thing.

I was taking everyone out to the Midnight Garden for dinner, drinking and some dancing. Noticing that the guys were holding their wives hands, I put mine across the back of the seat behind Selina and made sure my leg was lightly touching hers. She kept moving it over but really didn't have any room unless she started touching Steve's leg, so I had her there. Seeing her look up at me, I kept my eyes averted from hers. I could feel the annoyance radiating off of her. I'll let my little Princess have her day with her anger attitude towards me but my patience was starting to wear thin. By the end of the night, I plan on this attitude being a thing in the past. Bringing my mind back into the conversation, Denise congratulated me on finding someone like Selina to do amazing work in the company. Besides Geology, I found out that Selina loved the water, had her scuba diving credentials and planned on doing several dives with the team at Stone.

"That's not necessary," I blurted out loud.

"Excuse me?" Selina responded back to me with an edge to her voice. "This is what I do Mr. Stone. It's part of my job so I can see firsthand what is going on at the rig."

I saw Theresa and Denise both stare at me with matching frowns on their faces. This night wasn't going well for me right about now, I need a drink and to fix it.

"Let me explain Selina. I didn't know that you would be part of the dives and I have a complete team that handles that work for us. Forgive me for watching after your wellbeing."

"I can take care of myself Mr. Stone and have already connected with the team's Captain. I'll be doing my first dive with them tomorrow."

"Now that sounds exciting Selina," gushed Denise. "It must be an incredible world underwater. Now I am very envious of your job."

"I love excitement of diving, the serenity of the underwater world and the creatures that inhabit it. It's very calming."

"Well, I can see how you look forward to it," said Steve. "Our team is one of the best."

"I look forward to learning from them."

Listening to their conversation, I saw that we had arrived at the Midnight Garden. I made a mental note to be on the rig tomorrow when she was doing the dive. I wanted to be on hand if God forbid anything happened. I couldn't help but feel responsible and protective towards her. Now if I can only win her over.

DT opened the door and I moved out of the limo

first. Reaching my hand towards Selina, she made a slight hesitation before placing it in mine. As I helped her out of the car, I gave her a little smile and squeezed her hand. She was clearly not happy about the diving conversation. Now it's another error that I have to correct. Just as I suspected: Selina is strong willed and stubborn. I'll add in intelligent and incredibly sexy. Waiting for everyone to exit the limo, I told DT that we would probably be done by midnight but would text him if we were finishing up earlier.

Watching the women all go to the door together, Steve, Tom and I just stood there admiring them. The blonde, brunette and a redhead; all stunning women who had several other men just watching them enter the restaurant. I thought of Charlie's Angels as they walked ahead of us. I wouldn't put it past these three being able to run a country.

"We are lucky guys," said Tom.

"Yep," said Steve.

"I hope so," I added. "Let's go before some others move in for them."

Laughing together, the three of us walked into the restaurant. I saw several women looking at us too.

I could care less. All I could think about was the sexy woman in the magenta dress.

Chapter 19: Dinner Date/ Selina's Story

I couldn't help my heart racing out of my chest. I prayed Damien didn't hear it pounding away. He got out of the limo to meet me and I was ready to throw myself in his arms. That Armani suit with the crisp white shirt unbuttoned at the collar made me want him more than I ever thought possible. Oh God, I want to have his baby. It was insane, pure lust and something more that I didn't figure out yet or didn't want to. I remembered the body that was under those clothes and had to calm myself down just thinking about it.

 I kept to my program. Like Julia said, make him earn it and I plan on doing just that. I kept myself frosty towards him but knowing him the brief way I do, I know he was just appeasing me. He was a powerful man, a pure alpha male. He would accept my attitude only so far as he already stated that I was his. Well, I can play the game too. I knew this dress knocked him for a loop just by his reaction. His words to me were perfect for my answer. As my Boss, he shouldn't say those things to me but secretly I really loved it.

I tried to keep my leg from his when we sat in the limo but didn't have room to maneuver. I thought that maybe Steve kept his leg there so I couldn't move it. In fact, I was almost certain of it but God bless the girls. I knew I had Theresa and Denise in my corner, especially when Damien tried to assert his caveman tactics about me not going on the dives with the team. One thing that Damien will learn is that I take my job very seriously and everything that goes with it, I will be a part of. I won that battle.

Loving that he helped me get out of the limo, I made myself hesitate a brief second to give him a reason to think that just maybe I would get out of the limo myself, but I gave in. Another reason to feel his hand in mine was exciting. Even though it was a brief touch, I felt the current of attraction which I'm sure he felt as well.

Deciding not to wait for the guys, Denise, Theresa and I walked towards the entrance by ourselves for a fun night of dinner and dancing. We heard the music playing and the three of us were excited for a night out. Theresa whispered to me to play hard to get and not to worry. Denise agreed and the three of us turned on the charm to the doorman knowing that the guys were watching us. They would speak more to me when they had the chance but now we were going to just enjoy the evening.

As we walked into the restaurant, it was breathtaking. It was in a beautiful garden setting, hence the name Midnight Garden. The lighting was subtle and very romantic. There was even a water fall in the corner of the room with Koi fish swimming in the tank. Whoever designed this was a genius. Seeing that the guys caught up with us, I felt Damien stand by me as the Host greeted him. I was so attuned to him that I didn't even have to look to know he was there.

Our table was a little behind schedule which was fine with Damien. He informed the Host that we would be in the bar area for a few drinks. Walking us towards a beautiful bar area, I felt Damien put his hand on the small of my back to escort me to a table. His hand burned right thru my dress and marked me with his possessiveness. How would I get thru this meal with him so close to me? He seemed to sense my reaction to this as I caught his smirk as he looked down at me. Being a total gentleman, he pulled out his chair for me as did Tom and Steve for their wives. Taking charge ordering me a vodka/cranberry and a scotch for himself, this brought back memories and the trouble it got me in. I'll have one drink to relax and then have water for the rest of the night. As our drinks came to the table, Damien handed it to me as he clasped my fingers with his. My hand shook a little as I took the glass from him. I took several big sips of it, the alcohol hitting my stomach like a brick. Leaning over to me, Damien put his lips to my ear.

"Careful Princess, you know how you are when you drink."

I just felt chills down my body as his breath teased the sensitive skin by my ear. Looking at the girls, they gave me a little smile as they watched what was going on. My plan wasn't working but I had to stay the course. This man was the devil himself. He already had the right name, Damien, as in the

Omen series. He certainly was the devil come to life. I have to keep this professional.

At the right moment, Dawn said she had to use the ladies room and asked if Theresa and I would join her. Absolutely. I think I responded a little too enthusiastically but I have to get my balance back when dealing with Damien. Besides I needed to speak to the girls. Excusing ourselves, we made our way to the ladies room. Dawn checked under the stalls and said we were in the clear before Theresa started talking. This night was taking on a feeling of a covert operation.

"Listen Selina. We know what happened on the flight. Not all of the delicious details but we know. We also know that Damien has real feelings for you. Steve told us. We can also see that you have some kind of feelings for Damien too but you are fighting it. Good for you as it was shitty for him to do this to you but I understand why he did it."

"You sound like my friend Julia. I told her what I did on the plane and she was thrilled for me. I just had dumped my fiancé and well, she wanted me to have fun to get the asshole out of my system. Well, things just got out of hand on the flight.

God, Damien is incredible. I can't believe I just admitted that to the both of you. But he's my Boss!"

"If he doesn't care, why should you? You are both gorgeous together. I've known him a long time. Steve and Damien went to college together after Damien got out of the service. He has never acted like this with any other woman."

"That's for sure," agreed Denise. "It's almost comical to see him suffering and dying over you. Keep the hard act up a bit more; make him work for you and then just enjoy the fireworks."

"I saw him today in the deli with a blonde on his arm."

"Oh that tramp Lauren. They have been done for quite awhile but she is still clinging to him. Just watch out for her. I think she would stop at nothing just to keep him."

"On a serious note, we love Damien. We want him to be happy. He is married to his work because he hasn't found the right woman. I'm thinking you might be the one for him."

"Oh God." I just leaned my arms on the sink.

"We don't want to scare you, we are in your

corner, so are the guys but they will never admit it. Steve expected Damien to be sporting a black eye after the meeting today and joked around with him that he was playing with fire."

"Well I almost slapped him in the face but he caught my hand mid-way. I'm not proud of that at all. I've never reacted that way to anyone else."

"It's called passion Selina. Just go with it and we'll be here for support. Now let's get out there before the alpha's come looking for us."

I took a deep breath and then hugged my new found sister-hood friends. Pushing my shoulders back, I realized that the drink did go to my head a bit and thought maybe I will just ease up a bit on Damien. If what the girls were saying was true, then maybe he really is interested in me regardless of our positions in the company.

"Ready?" Asked Denise.

"Yes, can't wait," I smiled back at her.

While we were in the ladies room, the hostess moved us to the main dining room where we saw all three guys deep in conversation until we came back to the table. Standing up when we returned, I saw a new Vodka/Cranberry by my seat and thanked Damien for it. Rubbing my hand across his back, he looked at me with a frown on his face while waiting for me to sit back down. Two can play at this game and it was one I wasn't planning on losing.

"Thank you for my drink. It's just what I need." Damien just nodded his head at me and looked across the table at Steve. Seeing Steve shrug his shoulders, Denise elbowed him slightly in his rib and said something to him. I saw Steve smile at me from across the table. Let the games begin.

Chapter 20: Damien

Five minutes in the ladies room with those two vipers and a different Selina comes out of the bathroom. They all look like they are up to something but I'll just go for it for now. At least Selina doesn't look like she will stab me with her knife when I'm not looking. Quite the opposite. She seems to be warming up to me out of nowhere actually and this can't be good. Where Theresa and Denise are concerned, anything can happen. I run a company for God's sake. I can handle a slip of a woman who is gorgeous, sexy and brilliant. Really, who am I kidding? I'm going down with the ship. Catching myself laughing at my thoughts, I saw Tom frowning at me. Shaking my head at him, I mouthed the word Selina at him and he just smiled.

The waiter came over to take our order. I knew what I was having. Selina was staring at the menu with a second drink in her. As the waiter waited for her order, she turned her lovely eyes to me. "Damien, would you be so kind as to order for me?"

"Sure Princess. Seafood ok?" Seeing Selina nod, I told the waiter that she will have what I'm having. Our whole table ordered seafood as it was their signature meal. Hearing the band start to play, Tom and Steve escorted Theresa and Denise to the floor.

Standing up, I reached my hand down to Selina. "Dance with me."

Selina reached her hand into mine as I pulled her to me. I walked her out to the dance floor as the song "Lady in Red" was played. This couldn't be more perfect. Pulling her tightly towards me, she reached her hand up to my shoulder as my hand held her other hand close to my heart. She stared right at my collar, never venturing further than that until I called her name. I figured this was a good time to start my groveling.

"Selina, look at me." As she raised her gorgeous topaz eyes at me, I couldn't help but touch her cheek. "I will never regret what happened on our flight and what we shared together. I will never regret keeping from you who I was as it helped to bring us together even though it wasn't the most honest thing to do. I won't settle for anything other than having you in my life, as long as it takes, as long until you can trust me again. I don't care that I'm your boss. I just see an incredibly beautiful and intelligent woman in my arms that I want to know more than anything in my life. No matter what obstacles you feel are stopping us, whatever time you need to recover from your engagement, I will be as patient as I can. You are worth the wait Selina."

Seeing her emotions cross her face, I knew I struck a nerve within her. Holding her in my arms, we just danced across the floor. I knew we were at a pivotal moment if she was going to give us a chance or step away. As the song ended, I gave her a chaste kiss on her forehead. Seeing Tom and Steve look at me, I just gave them a slight nod to let them know I started my "groveling" with Selina. Holding her hand back to the table, I helped her sit back down as our dinner was served with another round of drinks. I saw the girls looking at her as Selina was quiet during the rest of the dinner. If I only knew what was going on her in mind about all of this.

Chapter 21: Selina

I knew the minute Damien took me out on the dance floor this would start to be the beginning of the end for me. I couldn't look at him at first as I knew I would have done something stupid like jump in his arms. I thought it would be safe to just stare at his collar and keep my eyes downwards from his. That is until he called my name…. The words he said to me, not regretting for a moment how he orchestrated our meeting and what happened with us on the flight; how he would never give up. These are all things women dream of; a man declaring his love for someone, putting aside everything just for them. I knew then that no matter what happened with my job, if I didn't try and have Damien in my life, I knew I would regret it for the rest of my life. If it didn't work out, then at least I had the experience of being with him. This is what I imagined it would be; what I thought I had with the fiancé but was so wrong about that man. And now this is scaring me. I have never felt like this with anyone before so throwing caution to the wind, I'm deciding to pursue whatever this is with Damien. If his Father and the Board find out about it, I could lose all credibility and possibly my job over him. Yes, Damien was worth it. I could always go back home and take that college teaching job.

I still wanted to think some things over and couldn't help but be a bit quiet over dinner. As I saw Damien looking at me, I reached my hand under the table and squeezed his thigh. I nodded my head slightly at him and then started to enjoy my dinner. Stealing a look back at him, I saw him wink at me as a slight smile lifted the corner of his lips. Feeling a weight being lifted off my shoulders, I was able to join the conversation with the girls and made plans to go shopping with them on Saturday with lunch right afterwards. It was nice to have new friends as well as have a potential boyfriend.

Once I decided to give us a chance, dinner took on a relaxed atmosphere for me. Joining in the lively conversation, I loved how the girls were outspoken and quite funny. It seemed like the six of us were friends for years. I was almost sorry for our evening to end.

Damien took care of the tab as Steve and Tom finished their after dinner drinks. Theresa told the guys we would wait outside for DT and get some fresh air.

"So it look like things are better with the both of you?"

"I'm going to give it a chance. I don't have anything to lose but my job and the rest of the heart," I said with a smile on my face.

"No one will find out Selina. We won't say anything, either will Steve or Tom. Just take things one day at a time with it and enjoy him. I guess Damien has started his groveling bit."

"Oh yeah, putting it on thick."

"Good, he knows he has to earn it."

"Just like the movie Jerry McGuire when she said "he had me at hello." Well Damien had me when he said he didn't have any regrets at what he did as it brought me to him."

"Good boy," said Denise.

As the door opened with the three guys walking out, DT just pulled up the limo. He just has impeccable timing as he jumped out of the car and opened the door for us.

"Your chariot waits."

"You are so charming DT," laughed Theresa.

"Hey are you flirting with our girls DT?" scolded Damien.

"Yes Boss. I kept them company for you and the others."

"Let's get everyone home then, shall we?"

I didn't know what would happen as we got to my complex. My heart was racing a bit with the anxiety starting to build. As Tom, Steve and their wives were dropped off, I wished them a good night and I told them I was looking forward to our Saturday shopping spree.

Damien told DT to head to my complex next as he

closed the glass divider to give us privacy.

"Nothing is going to happen Selina. As much as I want to experience what I know will be incredible with you, we have a big day tomorrow and you will be with the diving team. I will be on the boat monitoring everything from there." Looking at me with those intense blue eyes, he slowly lowered his face to mine. "And besides, I want to take my time with you and get back in your good graces." Licking my bottom lip from a mixture of nervousness and uncertainty, he reached out to touch it.

"Don't do that Selina. Let me."

Holding my arms over my head, he captured my lips with his. I couldn't move with his body pressing up to mine as he devoured my lips under his. With the feelings he was stirring deep inside me, I had to clench my legs together to keep from losing total control. Biting my bottom lip, he moved his tongue deep inside my mouth, teasing me and controlling me at the same time. I couldn't move my hands as I was held in place by Damien as his other hand took the liberty of exploring my body. He was pure dominance, not only in the boardroom but now with me. I was lost in the sensations he was creating. So much for making him earn it. I felt his hand on my inner thigh as he moved it higher until he felt the silk of my panties.

"God you are so wet already." Reaching around, he cupped my bare cheek as I like to wear thongs. I could feel the evidence of his desire for me pressed up against my thigh. "You are so beautiful Selina." Damien slowly lowered his hand from under my dress as well as slowly released my arms from over my head.

"This is not the time or the place for this. Tomorrow night, I'll make you dinner at my place. There are some things I want to discuss with you for business too. Bring a bathing suit." He gave me one of his sexy smiles as the limo slowed to a stop. Giving me a sweet kiss, he opened the door and helped me out of the car.

"See you at the rig tomorrow. Sweet dreams Princess."

Chapter 22 Damien

As much as I wanted to have Selina in my bed with me tonight, I wanted to give her breathing room from the last few days. There will be plenty of time to make her want me. We did have a big day ahead of us tomorrow. Parts of me were anxious about her diving with the team tomorrow. She was a scientist with an analytical mind. I'm sure she approaches relationships the same way. Coupled with a killer body and a beautiful face, she was a little less dangerous than TNT, well to me anyway. Watching her walk away from me into her complex, I waited until she was with security before I told DT to head on over to my place. I knew I wouldn't get much sleep tonight thinking of her under me while I possessed her body and soul. Of course it would be amazing but I will do the right thing for her. Make myself earn her trust; that's the only way this will all work.

I was home before I knew it and took out my phone. Pulling up Selina's number, I sent her a quick text.

Selina, thank you for a lovely evening. I enjoyed myself and hope you did too. See you tomorrow.
D

Not expecting a text back from her, I received one.

Damien, I did too. Thank you. See you tomorrow.
S

Smiling at the text, I knew I was on my way to being forgiven. Now time to take a cold shower.

Chapter 23: The Dive: Damien

"Good morning Mr. Stone," said Dave Michaelson, head of the diving team. "We are excited to have Dr. Harrison with the team this morning. I'm sure she will shed some light on the problems at hand."
"Dave, please make sure she is ok down there. I want the whole team safe, ok?"
"Sure thing Mr. Stone. Her diving credentials are all up to speed; she has done more dives than some on my crew. I'll be watching everyone and we'll take her lead to check the bottom. Here she comes now." We were all on a boat that had us

right at the base of the oil rig.

Around the corner came Selina with her wetsuit just on the bottom part of her body. She had on a black bikini top that seemed to barely cover her breasts. Her hair was up in a ponytail with no makeup on her face; she just took my breath away as well as caused an uncomfortable situation down below. Jesus, this woman will be the death of me.

"Good morning Mr. Stone. Good day for a dive. Hi Dave, are you all set with the team?"

I couldn't help but take in how adorably sexy Selina looked. She almost seemed to enjoy how uncomfortable she was making me feel as well as the look on Dave's face too as he was talking to her. This wasn't acceptable to me.

"Dr. Harrison, a word please."

Selina put her paperwork down and came over to me as I went to the other side of the platform.

"Selina, are you all set for this dive? Do you need anything else from me?" I caught her glance at my pants before her eyes met mine.

"No, not at this moment. I'm all set and looking forward to it." She gave me a little smirk, clearly enjoying this moment and I could take her comments in two ways.

"We can discuss your findings over dinner tonight then. Be careful down there."

"I'm always careful Mr. Stone." Hearing her voice being called, she turned away from me and she shrugged her arms into the wetsuit and zipped it up. She looked so sexy as the wet suit clung to all of her curves. I watched her put on the flippers and then the tank and mask. Making sure the tank was on and the correct levels were set, down came her mask and mouthpiece. As the team all gave each other the thumbs up sign, they disappeared over the back of the boat. Going up to the Captain's station, I was able to watch what was going on thru the TV monitors. They started sending back the images not only to us but also to Tom and Steve in the office. I was able to keep an eye on Selina as the divers went deeper into the Gulf. They had a half hour to send back all of the data so we could determine what we needed to do. I was counting down the minutes as I would feel better knowing the dive was over and Selina was back on the boat with me.

Checking the pylons, Selina pointed out a serious

crack in one that I'm guessing was caused by the shifting of the Gulf's floor. That can be repaired as it wasn't a major problem right now but if that cracked more and became unstable, we would have a serious problem on our hands. As the team dove deeper, they were taking photos of the floor where I saw Selina picking up rock samples from the bottom and putting them in a little sack attached to her waist. Grabbing her camera, she took images of the Gulf floor, concentrating on the area that she had brought to our attention during her presentation. I saw Dave swimming close to her, motioning to his meter that they had ten minutes to go, five of them would be to swim up to the surface.

Selina looked at her oxygen levels and pointed it out to Dave as she gestured wildly to him. We had no idea what was going on but I was becoming a bit concerned with their sense of urgency. Then we saw it. Dave sent an image back that showed her oxygen meter; Selina only had two minutes left in her tank. I felt the air knocked out of my lungs. This can't be happening. By my calculations, they had at least five minutes until they got to the boat.

With Dave grabbing her hand, he was swimming while practically carrying her. I noticed she didn't move her legs. What the fuck was going on?

"I need someone to tell me immediately what the Hell this means? Is Selina almost out of oxygen?"

"I'm guessing this is what is happening Mr. Stone, so Dave is swimming for them. They should have ten minutes left in their tanks. If she is almost out of oxygen, Dave is making her conserve what she has while doing the work for them. They are five minutes out sir."

Grabbing the counter, I couldn't take my eyes off the screen.

"Get the doctor up here with the first aid kit ready and the oxygen tank," shouted the Captain.

"Get a 911 call out to the paramedics on land to be waiting for us," I heard myself shout. "I want to know everything that has fucking gone wrong on this dive."

"Mr. Stone, look at the screen." The Captain and I both saw Dave putting his mouth piece into Selina's mouth for some oxygen and then switched back to him. Another one of the diving team joined their efforts, sharing their oxygen with

Selina too. She seemed to be lifeless between the two divers. My world was crashing down around me.

"Where are we time wise Captain?"

"Two minutes to go Mr. Stone. We will be ready to pick them up."

"She might not have two minutes Captain!"

The medic on the boat was already in position to administer first aid to Selina. All first aid equipment was ready and waiting. A text came in from Steve.

What the fuck is happening D?

Something happened with Selina's oxygen. She isn't getting anything.

Jesus. We'll call the paramedics on our end and get them to the dock. Let me know what happens. Hang in their D. She's a tough lady.

God I hope so.

"They are up, they are up! Pull Dr. Harrison up and clear out of the way."

Selina's lifeless body was pulled up over the side of

the boat. The boat's doctor and his assistant got right to work on her. I tried to get to her but was held back by two of the deck hands.

"I don't have a pulse. Chest compressions and charge it up!"

I just stood there totally helpless as the woman I've already lost my heart and mind to was lying there motionless on the boat deck. Everything was in slow motion as I saw them pulling down the zipper to get to her skin. As the doctors alternated together the chest compressions, I prayed.

I don't know how long it has been since I have prayed to the Almighty but I did. I hope He wouldn't decide to turn his back from me now as I have done for so many years to Him. It's funny that one turns to Him when there are dire circumstances but I was helpless to do anything else for her at this moment.

It was the only thing I had to give to her. I prayed for Him to bring her back to me. For the first time ever, this was a woman that I felt was a part of me; I have never felt this connection before with any of the women that came in and out of my life like a revolving door. Here is one that challenged me, could make me a better man and could give me LIFE.

"Clear!" The doctor zapped my Selina and I saw her body convulse with the electrical charge piercing thru her body. Checking for a pulse, the doctor shook his head. More compressions were being done until the machine was ready.

"Again, clear!"

Another zap went thru her body. Please Lord, bring her back to me. I can't lose her. I felt myself weakening under the stress. The relentless Damien Stone, being brought to his knees by this woman and a situation out of my control. At this point, I couldn't care what anyone thought. Please Lord, bring her back to me. I need her with me. You can wait for her. Please Lord, let me have her.

"We have a pulse! Oxygen now!"

Pushing a few of the divers away, I knelt down next to her as she started coughing into the mask. "Selina baby, please come back to me," I whispered into her ear. Seeing her eyes fluttering as they were trying to open, I shielded them from the blinding sun. Then those gorgeous topaz eyes focused on me.

"Damien," whispered Selina. I just bowed my head down in thanks and gratitude. Applause went up around the deck from the crew as the doctor just covered his face in his hands, the emotions just too overwhelming for words. I could give two shits what the diving crew and the Captain thought as I pressed my lips to her forehead. I needed her to know that I was right by her side and would never give up on her or on us. I felt her move her hand up to me as I clasped it firmly in mine.

"You will be fine now. Steve has the paramedics at the dock waiting to take you to the hospital for observation and treatment."

Hearing the Captain shouting orders to get us underway, I stayed right where I was next to her. Taking my phone out of my pocket, I talked a message into it to Steve, letting him know that Selina was with us and that we were getting ready to head back to shore. Then smiling down at Selina, I took the blanket that was handed to me to place it on her.

"What happened Damien?"

"Seems there was a malfunction with your oxygen tank. You only had two minutes worth of oxygen.

Dave swam both of you back to the boat and shared his oxygen with you. Another of the team came to assist too but you lost consciousness."

"How can that be Damien? My tanks were checked out by the crew as well as by me, twice. It doesn't make sense." I could tell Selina was getting really upset by this. Pushing her hair totally off her face, I told her to relax.

"Listen, let's get to the hospital and then we can figure this out. The main thing is you are here and I want you checked out, ok?"

"Yes Sir."

"I like the sound of that." I smiled down at my Princess but had an off feeling in the back of my mind that maybe someone did do something to her oxygen tank to sabotage this dive and I wanted that looked into immediately.

Chapter 24 The Hospital

Just as Steve promised, the paramedics were waiting for us the minute we docked. Bringing their stretcher, Selina was easily transferred into the waiting ambulance as I jumped into the back of it with her. Checking all of her vitals, the paramedics emailed all of their findings to the ER staff waiting for us to arrive. Modern technology at its finest. I would make sure Selina got the best care. I was advised she would be held overnight for observation anyway since this was a diving accident. Just as long as Selina was ok, then I could relax. I wanted the full report from the doctor and then we can talk about what happened with this dive.

I text Steve and Tom about what Selina had said to me. I had an unsettled feeling someone did try to sabotage this dive now and thought about the other various oil companies that also were drilling in the area. I hoped to God one of them wasn't that desperate to do this and put one of my team in harm's way. Selina could have easily died out there. Steve thought it was a good idea to reach out to our friend, Detective Samuel Peterson. It might be worth it to get something on record in case anything else happened in the future. Right now, I wanted to focus on Selina and to make sure that everything was ok.

"Damien, please go back to the office. I'm sure you have meetings to do. I'm going to be just fine.

Think of how this will look to your Dad and the Board of Directors." Selina had a point there but I will move at least one of the meetings.

"As an employee at Stone, it's my duty to make sure your wellbeing is taken care of after an accident. I'm sure my Dad and the Board will understand this and also be concerned about the nature of this accident." Lowering his mouth to her ear, Selina felt his breath cause goose bumps down her body. "And besides, there is no place that I want to be but here with you." Not wanting to alarm her, I wanted to let her know what Steve and I decided together.

"Selina, we are calling in a detective friend of ours, Detective Samuel Peterson to investigate what you have told me. I want to make sure this was purely an accident and not anyone trying to sabotage our work here." Selina just nodded as she shut her eyes.

"Ok Damien, I agree with this. Whatever I need to do, I will for you and the company."

The ambulance arrived without giving me a chance to say anything else to her. They whisked her away into the ER while I made arrangements with my assistant to cancel my 12pm appointment. Then I made arrangements for a private room for Selina. If she was going to have to stay here overnight, I wanted her to have privacy. As my phone started ringing, I saw that Steve was calling me.

"Hey D. How is Selina?"

"So far, so good. She is in the ER now getting checked out. I told her about Samuel and she will let him know anything she can tell him. I hope to God this is unfounded or we have a serious problem on our hands."

"Yeah, that's for sure. Your Dad already got wind of what happened and made an appearance here. I told him what I knew and he is waiting to hear back from you. He did make a comment that he found it strange that his son took such an interest in the dive this morning and maybe there was hope for you yet."

"Jesus Steve. I don't need his shit now."

"I'm sure he has it all figured out already D," chuckled Steve. "She's an attractive woman, you worked hard to get her here, I'm thinking he is putting two and two together."

"The main thing is Selina is ok but I have a bad feeling about this tank situation. I will feel better with Sam on the case and to get his opinion on this. Do you know when he can come to the hospital?"

"Anytime D. He is waiting to hear back from me."

"Ask him to come this afternoon. If this is foul play, we have to find out who did this, why they did this and press charges. Selina could have died out there. I can't put her or any others in danger."

"I hope you are including yourself in the mix D. You are our CEO. If the company is targeted, you can be too."

"Let's see what Sam says first Steve. Any one of us can be in danger. What a fucking mess. I feel like I've aged ten years."

"Go to her D. Make sure she checks out ok and what about her parent's? Do you think she will be in touch with them about this?"

"I don't know but what a way to meet the family." I looked up to see the doctor motioning to me.

"Look Steve, the doctor is calling me. Have Sam come by as soon as he can. I'll be in touch and will be in the office later this afternoon."

Hanging up with Steve, I practically run down the hallway.

"Mr. Stone, I'm Dr. Harper."

"How is she doctor?"

"The initial tests came back normal. We are just waiting on her blood tests and gave her a mild tranquilizer to take the anxiety away. She is upset as to what had happened and that is totally understandable in this type of accident. Do you know if she has family here?"

"No, everyone is in New Jersey. Is she asking for them? I can reach out to her parents."

"I would ask Selina first to see how she feels about that and work it out with her."

"When can I see her?"

"You can go in now. Selina was already asking for you. "

"I also want you to know that I have Detective Peterson coming to the hospital later this afternoon to speak to Selina about this accident."

"Just as long as he doesn't upset my patient, I will allow him to see her. I will have him removed if she becomes agitated."

"Fair enough Doctor. Thank you for all of your

help so far." I reached out to shake his hand but definitely wanted to get in the room with Selina. A huge wave of wanting to protect her came surging over me.

Chapter 25 Selina: Uneasy feelings

I keep going thru my mind all of the checks and rechecks with my tank. I was sorry to cause Damien any cause for concern but I'm not feeling good about this. Thinking that I could have died and never seen my family, friends and Damien shook me to my core. I felt a calmness come over me when the nurse came and administered the tranquilizer in my IV. It was mild enough to just take the edge off my anxiety but still enabled me to think things over a bit rationally about what had happened.

Oh my God! Damien! How was he when I was pulled on board unconscious? I felt a tear course down my face as I turned my head to stare out the window. It was then that I sensed him in the room with me.

"Selina," Damien said with a whisper.

Looking over at him, I felt protected and also something else. Love. How can that be? We hardly know each other. I watched him walk over to my bed and pull the chair close to me. Holding my hand, he wiped my tears away with his other hand.

"Well, saying that you scared the Hell out of me is putting it mildly Princess. I never want to relive that again."

"Damien, thank you for being there for me. I'm sorry that this happened and now that I have put a possible cause for concern with this dive. I just can't help but feel that something was deliberately done to my tank; maybe not to cause me serious harm or death but just to scare us from making new strides in drilling. It might have gone farther than the person or persons might have wanted this to go. I just can't shake this feeling." Fresh tears came into my eyes that I just couldn't help with all of the emotions surrounding me.

"Selina baby, if there is a threat here, Detective Peterson will get to the bottom of it. Now, I just want you to relax. All of the tests have come back normal; the doctor is just waiting for the blood results to come back. He feels that you will make a full recovery but you have to take it easy for now. I know that must be very difficult for you but you have to listen to the doctor and then to me too."

Damien gave me that beautiful smile of his and raised my hand to his lips for a kiss that I felt throughout my whole body.

"Do you want me to contact your family?"

"I was thinking about this because if there is some foul play here, then the news could get wind of it. I wouldn't want my parents and brother to hear about this on the news. Maybe I should call them."

"Ok, I'll step out to give you privacy then."

"No Damien, please stay with me. I might have to put you on the phone with one of my parents to answer questions I may not know the answers to."

As Damien dialed the number for me, I prayed that my Daddy would answer the phone and not my Mama.

Hearing my Dad's voice answer the phone, I breathed a sigh of relief.

"Hi Daddy," was all I could get out as I choked up on the phone. Damien held my hand to give me the strength to get thru this call.

"Listen, there has been an accident but I'm ok." I told him what had happened. He kept saying "ok" and "hmm" to what I was telling him. I told him how wonderful Damien was during all of this too and that I was staying in the hospital overnight for observation. Then he started in with his questions.

"So lass, do you think someone is out to do you and the company harm?"

"Maybe Daddy. You know how I am with my equipment. I wouldn't have missed this."

"And your boss, Damien is it? Sounds like he has been taking good care of you, maybe more than how a boss would take care of an employee? That much I have really gathered from this conversation my dear. Is he there with you now? May I speak with him?" Handing over the phone to Damien, I whispered that my Dad wanted to talk to him.

"Hello Dr. Harrison sir. Damien Stone here." It seemed that my Dad just wanted to hear from Damien what the doctor's reports were and if he felt I was in any danger. I heard Damien tell him that a trusted detective friend was coming by to interview me this afternoon. It seemed that my

Dad was satisfied that Damien was taking care of me so he asked to speak with me again.

"Such a self assured man Selina. You seem to be in very good hands. Now your Mama is here, frantic to speak to you. You don't have to sugar coat anything with her as she has been listening in on all of this conversation. She is very interested in Damien now that she knows you are ok. You take care of yourself and also Damien lassie."

"Yes Daddy. Hola Mama. Slow down Mama. Yes, I'm fine." Then I just lapsed into Spanish to be able to keep up with her conversation. Damien motioned that he would be right back as he saw Detective Peterson in the hallway. I went thru everything with Mama. She wanted to hear my voice tell the story. Finishing up my conversation with her, I promised to call her back tomorrow when I was released and she wanted to hear all about Damien too. Hanging up with her, I just had to take a deep cleansing breath. They said they would tell Sean Jr. I just didn't have the strength to go thru this again with him while I knew I would have to retell my side of the story to Detective Peterson.

"Selina, Is everything ok with your parents?"

"Yes Damien, I'm glad I told them. I would hate for them to find out from somewhere else."

Nodding his agreement, Damien made the introduction to his friend.

"Selina, this is Detective Peterson. Steve and I are friends with him so you can be totally comfortable with telling him anything about what happened and what you suspect."

"Hi Selina. I'm Sam Peterson. Damien filled me in on your concerns about what happened out at the rig. I'm happy to see that you are doing fine after this accident. I can assure you that if there is foul play involved here, I will find out for you and Damien. In the meantime, this stays between us and Steve, ok?"

"Yes, thank you Sam. Where do you want me to start?"

"How about who would have access to your tanks? I already have them in our possession and we are running prints on them. I'll get a sample of your prints so this way, forensics will separate yours from their findings."

So I gave Sam the list of names of the people on

the dive team with Dave being our team leader.

"Was he the one who helped you by swimming for the both of you and giving you part of his oxygen?"

"Yes, Dave did that for me."

"Damien, I've asked Steve for all of the film footage around the docking area as well as around your building. I just want to see if there is anyone suspicious hanging around the areas."

"That's fine Sam; whatever you need. If there is something wrong here, I know you will find it."

Sam asked me some more questions until the doctor came in and told him that he wanted me to get some rest.

"Of course doctor. Selina, you have been a great help. I have a lot to work with here. I will keep you and Damien up to speed on what we find out. Rest up and I'll speak to you when you are released."

Watching Damien walk Sam to the door, the nurse came in and checked my blood pressure and other vitals. I was so exhausted that I just wanted to take a nap. Damien came back over to me as my eyes struggled to stay open.

"Go to sleep Princess. I will come back tonight to

visit with you. You have my number if you need anything at all." Bending over him, he brushed his lips across my forehead. I watched his formidable figure walk towards the door as my eyes drifted to sleep. I could have sworn he stopped at the door to look at me again but I wasn't sure. I felt protected and cared for.

Chapter 26 The Girls

I'm lucky to have such good friends. After a good nap all afternoon, I definitely felt more myself. I felt sharper and a bit angry over what happened that morning.

I just finished talking with Julia when Denise and Theresa came barreling thru the door. They had flowers, a big Teddy bear, chocolates and a bottle of wine for them, slipping me a tiny sip to celebrate. After they listened to me as I told them what had happened, we said a quick prayer of thanks.

"I can only imagine how Damien was standing on the deck. Steve said he was a total mess," said Theresa.

"Listen, I think the groveling stage is long over,"

laughed Denise. "Poor man must have gotten grey hair from this."

"I thought about how he was when they brought me over the side of the boat. Even I get sick over the thought but now that's behind me and us. Where are the guys now anyway?"

"Well Steve and Tom are picking up BBQ and sneaking it into the hospital. You don't have diet restrictions so this calls for a celebration!" shouted Theresa.

"Did someone say a celebration!" laughed Steve as he carried in two massive bags of mouth watering BBQ. The smell was amazing and made me realize that I was hungry and certainly not for hospital food.

"I have the dessert," said Tom. I looked to the door at Damien who was just standing there staring at me. He looked so serious when everyone was in a jovial mood. I must have looked pathetic holding the Teddy bear in my arms when I really wanted to hold him in my arms. Holding out my hand to him, he crossed into the room and held onto it. I felt the electric current that seemed to go from him to me and back to him again.

Lowering his lips to mine, he clung to me desperately. I felt wave after wave of emotion in that kiss. Damien showed me his longing, the wanting and the almost sense of loss over what the outcome could have been. It was just Damien and me in the room together. The others left the room quietly to give us this time together.

I felt his tears fall gently on my face. This man, who was a rock in everything in his life, became so precious to me. I felt the desperation and longing in his kiss to me, the fear of almost losing me. It shattered me.

Pulling gently away from him, I wiped away his tears that were fresh on his cheeks.

"My turn." I gave him a watery smile. He knew what I meant by that from when he helped me on the plane and just gave me a smile that turned my insides out. I knew then that we were on the brink of sharing something very special between couples. Did I just think of us as a couple? Yeah I did and it felt good.

"Damien, I'm ok, let's put the accident behind us and figure out with Sam if this is something we need to worry about. Right now, you and I have friends here that are probably starving and want to just celebrate with us."

"When you get out of here, we have to talk."

"I know." He bent over to give me another kiss when the door opened and Steve stuck his head in.

"Can we eat now? The troops are getting restless."

"Sure Steve, let's celebrate," said Damien.

Two hours later, the doctor came in to kick everyone out. My nurses and aides were all in my room, really causing a commotion that the doctor wasn't pleased about. He wasn't worried about me but about the other patients on the floor. Tom gave him a pulled pork sandwich which softened his mood but he still kicked everyone out. The girls insisted we were still on for shopping on Saturday and I promised them I would be there. As everyone filed out, Damien was the last to leave. His eyes just bored into mine until he gave me that sexy eyebrow lift and a quirky smile.

"Yes Mr. Stone. What are you smirking about?"

"Well good Doctor, I'm thinking about how sexy you are, even in that hospital gown and knowing you are naked underneath it."

"Get out of here Damien. How can you even think about that now?"

Coming closer to the bed, he put his face and lips close to mine.

"I'm thinking how good it will be when I'm in you and make you mine. You know it's just a matter of time before that happens Princess."

Taking a deep breath, I reminded him that we have to talk first.

"Yes, we will but now, you need your rest. I'll be here in the morning to take you to my place to recover."

"That's totally not necessary Damien."

He cut me off and let me know his assistant already packed a small suitcase of clothes and toiletries.

"Yes, you will be staying at my place. You can recover there. I have a housekeeper that will keep an eye on you. Until we know what we are dealing with here, I don't want you alone in your condo. You are safer with me."

How safe could I be with Damien? My heart started racing at the thought as I knew I was already in danger of losing myself to him.

"I'm giving you the rest of the week off. You can do your research at my house. I just want you safe, ok?"

"Yes Mr. Stone."

Hearing over the loud speaker that visiting hours were over, Damien leaned over for a kiss. I felt my heart pounding in my ears at the thought of his lips on mine. He did not disappoint. With his lips slanting across mine, he pulled me close to his chest. I felt my breasts respond to his masculine hardness. I know that Damien felt this too. Before my thoughts turned towards doing things that I wasn't ready for yet, Damien pulled back from me and gave me a sweet kiss on the lips.

"Now get some rest and I'll see you in the morning. If you need anything, give me a call, ok?"

"Yes Damien, thank you for everything."

Chapter 27   She's home

I picked Selina up from the hospital as planned and got her settled into my home. I needed to get into the office for meetings all day, one of them with my Father. It was something I certainly didn't look forward to.

"Selina, if there is anything you need, you can call down to the front desk and they will get it for you. Just relax, watch Netflix and work if you want. I'll be home as soon as I can."

"I'm not sick and really can go to work."

"I'm ordering you as your Boss, to take this week. Until we know what's going on, I want you safe." Pulling her against me, I smoothed a piece of hair away from her face and lightly tugged on her ponytail to move her face up closer to mine. I noticed that she moved closer to me as she pressed that sexy body right up next to mine.

"It's better knowing you are safe here than at your place. Besides, I like having you here."

Smiling down at her, I took her lips on mine. Hearing her whimpers of desire, I turned this kiss into something that didn't need to begin right now. I couldn't get enough of her, couldn't get close enough to her. Her sundress and my suit separated us when all I wanted to do was make her mine. Moving my hands under her dress to her thighs, I slowly moved the up to grasp that cute ass of hers and squeeze her. My lips trailed down her neck as I felt her arms wrap around my neck. Picking her up against me, she held on around my neck with her legs around my waist. Pushing her up against the wall, Selina was aware of how much I wanted her. As she tipped her head back, I enjoyed the soft texture of her skin and felt her heartbeat beneath my lips. Nipping at her collar bone, I knew this was getting out of hand. It wasn't what I would want for our first time. She deserved more than that.

Lowering her gently to the floor, I put my forehead to hers.

"I have to go. God knows that I don't want to but this isn't happening now. I don't want meetings and deadlines to stop me from enjoying you as much as I would love that right now."

Selina just nodded her head in agreement. I touched her by her chin as I moved my thumb across her bottom lip.

"God you are so beautiful." I hugged her to me as though she was my last breath. This woman had the power to destroy me.

 "Ok, I have to go and will call you later."

I hated leaving her. DT was waiting for me at the

curb to rush me into work. Just knowing Selina was safe at the condo made me relax a bit until we figured out what happened yesterday. I couldn't shake off the uneasy feeling of waiting for the other shoe to fall. Call it my military training or just intuition but something wasn't right here. Going thru emails, I saw call coming in. Mom. My Mom, who doesn't take no for an answer, insisted that she go by the house later with food for lunch and to meet Selina. I warned her that I would disown her if she made Selina uncomfortable.

"Now, why would I do that son, especially if she is the girl that is stealing my son's heart. Is there something here that you need to tell me?"

Really not wanting to share anything with her just yet, I told her in no uncertain terms no. I could tell she didn't believe me. Mothers have a knack of figuring when their sons are keeping something from them. I felt like I was a 10 years old again and getting into all kinds of trouble.

"Damien love, your secret is safe with me. It's your Father you need to worry about."

"I've been avoiding him."

"It's obvious. Just talk to him. To Hell with the

Board and what they might feel about this. In the meantime, please let Selina know I'll be at your house say around noon with a delicious lunch. God knows hospital food is not the most appetizing." Hanging up abruptly on me so it didn't give me a chance to argue with her, I called Selina to let her know that my Mom would be by at noon.

"No problem Damien. I'm looking forward to meeting her. I'll start working out all the data from yesterday too do we don't lose any time."

"Ok. I'll call you later."

Chapter 28 The Meeting

"Dad how are you?" I strode forward into my office as I saw my Father standing by the windows. Standing at 6'3, we were practically identical in height and looks. Let's just say I know what I would look like say in about twenty-five years. He still commanded respect when he walked into a room and I could tell by his stance, this was going to be a conversation I'm was not going to like. I'm trying very hard to keep my anger in check but was slowly losing control of it.

Reaching for my phone, I called my assistant. "Anna, please hold all calls." Slamming the door, I turned to him and got ready for this confrontation.

"Has Steve gotten you up to speed on what happened yesterday?"

"Yes. How is Dr. Harrison?"

"She is fine and already working on her report from her findings."

"Good. Where is she Damien?"

"She's safe at my condo. Until we find out what Sam discovers, I felt it was best that she is protected in case this was an incident to harm her."

"Damn it Son! The Board is already buzzing with rumors that you are sleeping with the girl. You are the CEO for God's sake. You need to set a prime example to the staff about not fraternizing in the workplace."

"First of all, I'm not sleeping with her Dad. I respect her as a colleague and for the work she has accomplished in her life. Second, it's no one's fucking business, yours included, what goes on behind my closed doors and personal life. And third, Selina almost died out there on my watch. We are trying to determine if this was an intentional act of sabotage and attempted murder on one of our staff. So I don't need you or anyone else to dictate to me how I decide to protect one of my staff, are we clear on this?"

"Enough Damien! We can argue this shit until we are both blue in the face. Damn it Son. I'm not going to start a fight with you over this. You are a smart man and know how the Board can be. I'll dispel any rumors with them as best I can and tell them what you have told me." I saw my Dad walk over to the windows as he pushed his hands thru his hair.

"Ok Damien, now I'm speaking to you as your Dad and not one of the Board. I want you to tread carefully. I can see that you have feelings for this girl; God knows your Mom and I are happy about this. We never thought we would ever see the day. Just take this one day at a time and discretion please."

"Ok Dad."

"Now your Mom has plans to bring Selina lunch today and to meet her."

"That's the plan." I couldn't help but feel put off by the fucking Board. My Dad represented them but right now, he was my Dad. I recognized what a hard role he had to play in this.

"Son, I want you to be happy. You deserve it after everything that you have done with your life. She seems to be the right woman to be at your side; and maybe someone who can handle you," he chuckled.

"Thanks Dad." Giving him a handshake and hug, I walked him to the door as he left. Now with that behind me, I could get on with my day.

Chapter 29 Mrs. Stone

So as noon came closer, I put the finishing touches to my appearance. Anna brought my favorite jeans and I paired that with a cute peasant type blouse. I kept my hair back in a pony tail as I love to keep my hair back when I work. As for my makeup, I kept that to a minimum. I already had a nice glow from the sun. I wanted Mrs. Stone to like me for me. Hearing the buzzer and seeing it was noon, I told security to please send her up.

Taking a deep breath, I opened the door to a beautiful woman. About my height and blonde hair, Mrs. Stone was a striking figure.

"Selina, so nice to meet you."

"It's so nice to meet you too Mrs. Stone." I looked behind her at the security guard as he was carrying a few bags of groceries.

"Thank you my dear and please call me Evelyn. None of this Mrs. Stone stuff."

I already liked her as she was so personable. Helping the guard with the bags of groceries, I couldn't help but notice that this was more than lunch.

"I brought you and Damien some additional food, steaks, potatoes, veggies, yoghurt, cookies and some other things. I know he doesn't want you even venturing out of this condo for your own safety. It's scary for right now, just until Sam can weed out things. Ok, now let me look at you." I felt Evelyn's eyes take in everything about me, almost to the point of being uncomfortable.

"Now I know why my son likes you. You are a beautiful woman inside and out. Things have a way of working out as there are no such things as coincidence. Everything happens as it was meant to be." I lived by that mantra too. I believe in destiny and thought back to everything that happened to bring me to this point; to bring me to Damien.

"I know how my son met you. Though I raised him better than that, I can now understand his motive. I hope you have forgiven him my dear."

I couldn't help but turn a nice shade of red. She didn't know everything that happened on that flight or did she? How embarrassing.

"Yes, Evelyn, I have. I couldn't stay mad at him for long as he is very charming and persuasive."

"Yes he is. So is his brother, Richard, but he can be a tad more serious than Damien. Dawn is just like Damien, strong willed and outspoken. I would love you to come to dinner one night to meet everyone."

"I would love that, thank you."

I have to say, I had a beautiful lunch with Evelyn. We spoke about what happened on the dive, my work, her volunteer work which I told her I would love to get involved in and my family. Before I knew it, she needed to leave. Damien's Dad was almost done with his golf game and she was going to join him at the club. I thanked her so much for her visit, for lunch and the extra groceries.

"It was so nice meeting you my dear. I hope to see you very soon again and enjoy each other's company. And Selina, one thing: forget about your jobs and the Board. One needs to follow their journey and see where love takes them." Giving me a wink, Evelyn let herself out of the condo. Closing the door behind her, I realized that Damien's family was very close, just like mine. The thought of possibly being a part of his family gave me a good feeling as I missed mine so much. I wonder if I can get any of them to visit me soon, even my brother if my parents couldn't get away. Thinking of waiting until Christmas to see them was just too far away. The sound of the intercom brought me out of my thoughts.

"Dr. Harrison, you have a package that was just delivered. I'm sending someone up with it, ok?"

"Yes, of course."

Wondering what that could be, I looked thru the peep hole at the security guard standing there with a white envelope.

"Dr. Harrison, this was left for you." Thanking the security guard, I was curious as to who had this sent to me. No one knew I was here but a handful of people.

So I carefully opened it up and a chill came over me. It read:

Stay away from Stone industries and Damien or else. I'm watching you.

Dropping the letter on the counter, I picked up my cell and called Damien immediately.

"Hi Princess."

"Damien, who knows I'm staying here?"

"My parents, Sam and Steve. Why?"

"The security guard said that an envelope was delivered to my attention here. I opened it up and there was a threatening note in it that says stay away from Stone Industries and you or else."

"You have got to be fucking kidding me?"

"I wish I was."

"Ok, don't touch the letter any more in case there are fingerprints on it. I'll call Sam and get him over there as fast as he can. I'll call the guards downstairs and see if they remember anything or if they have anything on the security cameras. Did they happen to say who delivered the note?"

"I didn't ask them. I really wasn't thinking about that, just thinking about who knows that I'm here."

"Obviously someone is watching you. Don't go anywhere. I'll get there as soon as I can. I'll call Sam now. Jesus Selina. What the Hell is going on?"

"I don't know Damien but I'm scared and pissed at the same time."

"That's my girl. I promise you we'll get to the bottom of this. Just lock the door and stay in the condo."

As I hung up with Damien, I thought about how quickly my life has changed. I went from a broken woman to having sex with a stranger on a plane who has turned out to be my boss who is very attracted to me: to me almost dying to possibly being on my way to loving her boss. On my way to loving? No, I was already there. I am in love with Damien. I know for sure that in a short time, this is who I was waiting for in my life. We have gone thru more in less than a week then what some couples go thru in a lifetime.

I'm worried that I'm putting Damien in danger being with him now. What do I do? Do I forfeit my happiness to protect him and his company? Who is this person who doesn't want me around? Could this be the same person who might have tampered with my tanks on the dive? If they are, they are very capable of doing anything to get what they want. If they want me out of the way, they would do it. Keeping my reservations of being with Damien to myself, the intercom startled me out of my thoughts.

It was Sam. I let him up and waited anxiously for him to arrive.

"Selina, Damien called me immediately. Let's see it."

"Here it is Sam. I was careful to just touch the corners. I'm hoping you can get some answers very soon as this note puts me on edge a bit. Only a handful of people know I'm here and I can't see any of them causing a problem for me."

"We have an idea who is doing this but I need them to slip up. I haven't told Damien anything yet but I may need you to help us flush out the person or persons doing this."

"This sounds like a police drama with me caught in the middle."

"Yes, I agree but sometimes this is how these things go down. I'm going to take this note with me and try to lift a print from it. I don't believe this is an act of a professional criminal so you can breathe a sigh of relief there. In the meantime, you are not to leave this place under any circumstances. I'll have an unmarked car downstairs watching the place. The guards already know so they are on alert. One of the guys was someone who worked with me on the force. You are well protected."

He looked at me as though knowing what was in my thoughts.

"Selina, if are you planning on leaving Damien because of this, he will find you. I can see the look in your face. I will find out who is threatening you, I promise you this. Walking away from Damien will not be the answer. I know that man all too well. He would go thru fire for you." Winking at me, the man of my dreams walked into the condo. Not even acknowledging Sam, he came over to me and just held me.

"Um Damien, let the poor girl breath," chuckled Sam.

Looking down at me, those blue eyes drowned me in emotions.

"Are you ok?"

"Yes now that you are here." Nodding his head at me, he turned to Sam with an attitude that was pure Damien.

"Sam, let me see the note."

"Don't touch it D. I'm taking it over to the lab and I also told Selina, I have an unmarked car downstairs for observation. The guys downstairs are aware of what's going on so Selina will be under 24 hour surveillance."

"Damn it Sam. Are you close to finding the bastard that is doing this?"

"Not yet but one thing is for sure, they are not professional. Checking with our underground sources, there is no threat or target to either of you or the company."

"Selina, I'll be right back. I just want to walk Sam out."

As I watched Damien close the front door behind him, I realized at that moment if God forbid something happens to me, I want to have known Damien. That means everything. Knowing that I have moments to spare, I run into the spare room with my decision that I wanted him. Looking in my bags, I saw that Anna packed my sexy new lingerie that I picked up at Maddie's. God bless Damien's romantic assistant.

Letting my hair down in waves, I put the black lingerie slip on and planned my seduction. Hearing the door shut, I came out of the room only to be standing in front of Lauren!

"What the Hell are you doing in here?"

"I can ask the same of you too. What are you doing, slutting your way to the top? Damien is mine, not yours."

As she is talking to me, I see a glint of a knife in her hand and also a wild unstable look in her eye. I felt my heart speed up as the adrenaline flowed thru my body. Where did Sam and Damien go?

"Answer me this Dr. Harrison. Why have you spoiled all chances for me to marry that man? Look at you just standing there, just waiting to be fucked. Well, that's not going to happen good Doctor. You know, I ought to scar that pretty face of yours so Damien won't even look at you. Then he will be in my bed where he belongs and not crawling after you." Lauren starts slashing the knife thru the air as try to remain calm but I'm at the very brink of hysteria now. I just knew I had to keep talking to her to distract her. I felt the tears start to flow down my face.

"Lauren, why don't we just talk about this? I didn't know you felt this way about Damien. You don't have to do anything you will regret. Please don't do this Lauren!"

The laugh that echoed thru the condo was eerily like a woman that was insane or definitely on her way to being insane. I didn't take my eyes off of her eyes.

"You should have died out in the Gulf. How you ever survived that is a miracle." Seeing Damien, Sam and a few of the guards walking quietly thru the front door, I wanted her to keep talking while they decided what they were going to do.

"Oh my God, did you have something to do with my accident?"

"I had help of course. I couldn't do it on my own. So I gave him money and let him fuck me. Dave was putty in my hands. He said it was nothing to hit a valve to let some air out. He really didn't care about you. No wait! I take that back. He thought it would be a waste to kill you as he wanted to fuck you first. You are like Helen of Troy: all of the men seem to want you but I wanted you out of the way permanently. You can't have Damien. I won't let you. So now it looks like I will have to do the job myself." Lauren started to make her move towards me as I backed up down the hallway.

I knew that Sam had enough evidence with Lauren's confession but I wanted to see if I could try to reason with her and come out of this without getting hurt or killed.

"Lauren listen to me. I'll leave. I'll pack up and catch a flight today to go back home. You can have Damien. That's what you want, right? You do this, you will go to jail for the rest of your life so where would you be then?"

"You would still be alive and who is to stop him from chasing you back to the East Coast. No, I will have to kill you."

Seeing Damien, Sam and the guards making their move, Sam was the first to react.

"Drop it Lauren or I'll shoot. It's over. Drop the knife now and put your hands in the air. Do it now," shouted Sam.

"I hate you Doctor. I hate that you have taken my man away from me."

"Lauren," said Damien. "You haven't lost me. I'm here for you. Please put the knife down and come here to me."

As Lauren still stared at me, she addressed Damien.

"This woman ruined my chances with you my love. With her out of the way, you would love me, marry me and we would have lots of children together. We would be the dream power couple in the business world. I would love that."

"Lauren, leave the Doctor alone and we'll start our lives together today, just you and I. But you have to drop the knife. If you kill her, you will go to jail for the rest of your life and we'll never be together. Do you understand me?"

Waiting for her answer seemed like an eternity.

"You're right Damien, she isn't worth it."

Dropping the knife on the floor, she turned and walked over to Damien with a twisted smile on her face. As soon as she got closer, Sam and one of the guards grabbed her from behind and pinned her down to the floor. My legs gave way as I felt myself sliding down the wall. I heard hysterical crying sounds and realized it came from me. Damien ran to me and scooped me up in his arms. Holding me close to his body, my sobs wracked thru my body at the thought that I could have died again. I heard him whispering words in my ears but for the life of me, I didn't know what he was saying. I felt an enormous sense of comfort in having someone take care of everything for me right now.

Bringing me into his bedroom, he sat me carefully on his bed and put his bathrobe around me.

"It's over Princess. I will not let anything happen to you. Stay here for one second and I'll be right back, ok?"

Nodding my head yes, I crawled to the center of the bed into a ball and just hugged myself. Smelling Damien's scent on his robe and on the pillow comforted me but I needed his strength right now. Crying everything out of me, my breakup, the flight, the dive, meeting him and wanting him, I finally felt stronger than I have in a long time.

Chapter 30 Damien: Safe at Last

Hearing Sam tell his partner to find Dave, I looked over to Lauren who was cuffed and secured with one of the officers guarding her.

"Lauren, why couldn't you just move on? Why this?"

"You have ruined me for all men Damien. When she came on the scene, I saw how you looked at her. I knew then that I lost you."

"You lost me long before Selina came here. I can't help but feel pity for you Lauren. I hope you will be able to get the help you need."

"What help Damien? I'll be out soon and we can plan our wedding. I don't care if I get pregnant before we are married too. I might even be carrying your baby now!" She started the wild uncontrolled laughing again. It's a sound I don't think I will ever forget.

"Get her out of here," Sam shouted to the officer. As we watched the officers and guards leaving with Lauren, she was singing that nursery rhyme about two people in a tree kissing.

"Thank you Sam for everything. I don't know how I could ever repay you."

"We suspected Lauren was behind this but didn't want to say anything yet. Having her give up Dave was an added bonus."

"I'm sick over that. He was a good man or so I thought. He even tried helping with getting Selina back to the boat by sharing his own oxygen."

"Well what Lauren offered him is a temptation to some men. It's sick. And it sounds like he grew somewhat of a conscious by sharing his oxygen. I'm sorry you had to hear that he wanted Selina too. We'll get him picked up too and off the streets. Both of them are facing attempted murder charges now. I hope Lauren was worth it to him as they will both go away for a long time. We'll need statements from both of you but right now, go to Selina."

"You don't have to tell me twice. Thank Sam. I owe you one."

Locking the door behind Sam, I took off my jacket and sent a few messages.

Texting Anna, I told her I'm out for the rest of the day and to cancel my meetings. Then I called

Steve. I told him quickly what happened and that I was taking the rest of the day to be with Selina. He promised to hold down the fort and fill Tom in on what happened. I figured I would talk to my family later on but right now, I just wanted to be with Selina. Shutting off the cell, I walked into my bedroom. Selina sat up holding my robe tightly around her. With her hair tousled and tear stained face, she held her hand out to me. She never looked more beautiful but I knew I had to possess her, to take these horrible memories from the last few days away from her.

Not taking my eyes off of her, I took off my tie and ripped open my shirt, not giving a shit that buttons flew all over the room. I needed her now as I know she needed me. Selina stood in front of me and carefully took off my belt and then my pants. As I kicked off my shoes, she took my robe off herself. She went to take off her lingerie but I stopped her.

"Let me do this. I need to do this."

Pulling her close to me, I kissed my way from her jaw line down to her neck. My lips bit and licked the sensitive part between her shoulder and neck.

Hearing her sweet sounds made me hard just thinking of making her mine. Putting my fingers in the straps of her lingerie, I slowly pulled them down as I looked deep into her eyes. My fingers lightly touched her nipples as they came alive under my fingertips. I could feel myself get harder just by doing this. Pushing her lingerie all the way off, she just stood there in her black lace thong. She was mine.

"Selina, you are so gorgeous."

" I need you Damien. Please don't make me wait."

That was my undoing. Picking her up, we both fell into my bed with a desperation that knew no bounds.

I feel like we've lived a lifetime already. With a sense of desperation, I tore off her panties. We were both running hot that there was no way of turning back.

I had to know her. Pushing her legs apart, my hands moved up the inside of each thigh as Selina writhed underneath me. This woman was made for me and I planned on showing her just that. Leaning over her, I captured a nipple between my lips, sucking on it as my hand caressed the other one.

"Oh God Damien," cried Selina.

Placing kisses all the way down her stomach, I made my way between her legs. I saw that she was ready for me but I wanted to savor this time with her. Moving my fingers thru her folds, she instinctively lifted her hips to find the pleasure that only I can give to her.

Grazing my fingers against her clit, I slowly teased her at her opening. Hearing her whimpering cries, I moved them into her. God she was so wet.

"What do you want Selina? Tell me."

"I need you Damien. Please," begged Selina.

Moving my fingers in and out of her, Selina pushed against my hand, searching for her release. It wasn't going to happen this way. Pulling my fingers out of her, I heard her cry out for more. Putting my lips against her clit, I stroked her with my tongue until Selina was thrashing on the bed. I felt her getting closer as I put my fingers back inside of her. I wanted her to feel my love for her, the desperation of what we could have lost. I couldn't get enough of this sweet lady and wanted to show her how good we were together.

"Please Damien. I can't wait any longer."

"Come for me now Selina." That's all she needed to hear as she screamed my name over and over again as waves of pleasure passed thru her body. Pulling her legs over my shoulders, I didn't wait for her tremors to still but pushed my way into her. God she felt so tight. Selina gasped at the shock at me being inside of her. Moving within her, I kissed her deeply as she held my face between my hands. Sitting back, I brought her up with me as she was fully impaled on my cock.

"Oh my God Damien," Selina wept. Moving faster inside of her, I felt her squeezing me as we were both getting close to what we needed together.

"Not yet Selina. Wait." I lowered my head to suck on one of her nipples as Selina threw her head back. Our sweat slicked bodies clung together as Selina gripped onto to my shoulders. She was moving her hips so seductively as I pumped myself into her like a man starving for love.

"Damien please, I'm going to come. I can't wait any longer."

"Then do it babe."

Throwing her head back with her neck exposed to

my lips, Selina screamed once again. Following her, I felt my love pour into her. I never had a reaction like this with anyone else. She kissed me deeply, taking my moans into her mouth while grabbing onto my hair. I touched her clit and brought her to another orgasm. This seemed to go on forever until we both lay side by side, with me still deep inside her. Holding her against my body, I wrapped my arms around her middle with my hand playing with her nipples. This was an amazing woman; loving and giving. Putting my face into her neck, I started kissing her as she started giggling.

"That tickles."

"You loved it when I was inside you."

"Yeah but this is the after effects. It feels so good."

"You feel so good Selina." I felt myself growing hard again. I knew I would never have enough of this woman and continued to show her this thru the night.

Chapter 31 Selina: Aftermath

Slowly awakening from a night of passion with Damien, I felt an arm lying possessively around my waist. I was a bit sore but it was a good sore as Damien loved me throughout the night. I heard him lightly snoring by my ear and savored this time together with him. I knew I had to get up and get to the office, even though my "Boss" wanted me to stay home for the rest of the week. I had work to do from the dive, especially work on that rig to keep it safe for the men working out in the Gulf. Moving slowly from under Damien, I went into the bathroom to take a hot shower to get the kinks out. I winced a little when I felt the soreness between my legs. I've never had a lover like Damien or really as endowed as he was too. Smiling to myself, I just felt so incredibly happy. Lauren was locked up and I'm sure by now Dave was too. The only thing that worries me is what the Board might do if they find out about the both of us. Surely we are allowed a private life if it doesn't interfere with our jobs. I was so caught up with my thoughts that I jumped when Damien pulled me against him.

"Good morning love," said Damien as he pushed himself up against me. I felt his cock fully come to life as he rubbed up to me. Turning in his arms, Damien kissed me with such passion that it took my breath away. This man knew how to kiss! Picking me up, he slammed his cock deep inside me and pushed my body up against the shower wall to help hold me up. Moving deep inside me, every movement brought me closer to the brink of release. I never thought I could feel the love I have for this man. Holding onto the shower head, this brought my tits to his mouth as he latched onto a nipple like a man starving for it. Biting down on it and then licking it made the feeling go right to my clit. Pain and pleasure; a powerful combination. I wanted more of that.

"Please Damien, don't stop."

"My girl loves that." Grabbing the other nipple into his mouth, he bit down again and swirled it in his mouth. It was more intense as I threw back my head and moaned out loud.

"Come for me Selina," commanded Damien.

Moving deeper within me, I felt a buildup of

emotion, a tidal wave of pleasure that came crashing down on me. I held on to Damien for dear life as I felt like I was drowning in his love as I felt him getting bigger inside me.

"Oh God Selina, you are mine," Damien shouted as he spilled himself into me. As I felt him coming inside me, it set off another orgasm that ripped thru me as I bit into his shoulder and cried out into his neck. As our breathing came under control, Damien slowly lowered me to the shower floor as I just clung to him. I didn't trust my legs to hold me up and thought he must feel the same way as he leaned against the shower wall.

"You really know how to wake a man up in the morning love."

"Look who's talking." I reached up to touch the muscles of his chest and that beautiful tattoo that draped over his body. Damien was a work of art, right down to his cock. And he was mine. He smoothed my hair from my face and kissed me so gently that he brought tears to my eyes. I so wanted to tell him that I loved him but held that back from him. I felt it was too soon to share that just yet.

As we both washed each other, I felt kisses across my shoulder blades and down my back. He ran his hands over my buttocks and leaned down to kiss each one. Sighing from how good it felt, Damien's lips trailed back up my back to my neck until he turned my head and reached for my lips. Clinging onto him, I kissed him back with all of the emotion I had inside of me, needing to reach deep into his heart and soul. He ran his hand down my stomach in between my legs and massaged my hungry clit. Only for this man was I capable of doing what I have been doing and responding as only he can make me. It was like we couldn't get enough of each other. Teasing me with his fingers, I opened my legs wider for him. Hearing him groan in my ear, he lightly bit the lobe as his mouth traveled down my neck. Oh God, he knows exactly what my body loves already. How is that possible? Turning my body towards his, he dropped to his knees and lifted one of my legs over his shoulder. Pushing his tongue deep inside of me, he fucked me with his tongue as his finger played with my clit. I was going to come again. I couldn't believe my body was capable of this but it was responding to Damien. He controlled me. As though knowing I was close, Damien grabbed hold onto my nipple and twisted it as his fingers were buried deep inside me. Sucking on my clit put me over the top. "Damien! Oh my God!" I yelled out as I held his head close to me. Wave after wave of pleasure moved thru me. I was shaking from the force of it. Damien made sure I enjoyed every moment of the pleasure he gave me. As soon as I could stand, I wanted to give him the same pleasure he gave me. Stroking his cock, I knelt down in front of him and kissed the crown of it. Tasting him already, I slid my mouth down the length of him. Sucking him and teasing him with my tongue, he started to move into my mouth.

"That's it baby. Take it all."

I relaxed my mouth so I could take all of him down into my throat. I heard Damien moan in pleasure. Using my hand to touch the full length of him as I moved up and down him, I felt him getting larger. I knew he was getting near so I moved faster.

"You are a greedy young lady, aren't you?"

Looking up at Damien, I gave him a sassy wink and moved faster on his cock.

"Selina," Damien moaned as he gripped the back of my head. Throwing his head back, I felt him shoot into my mouth as I swallowed everything he gave me.

"Oh God baby." I felt the last drops come into my mouth as I lovingly gave him a few more licks and then kissed the top of it.

Pulling me up to him, he kissed me long and deep until we realized that the water was cool to the touch.

"I think we used up all the hot water in the building," smiled Damien. Shutting off the water, he wrapped a towel around me and then himself. Picking me up, he carried me to bed and lay down next to me. Pulling the comforter over us, I felt the tug of a nap closing in on me.

"Don't you have to go into the office."

"I'm the boss and I'm deciding to take a sick day with you." Snuggling deep next to him, I felt my eyes close, safe and warm in the arms of my love.

Chapter 32 Confrontation

As I slowly woke up, I heard Damien on the phone with someone. I couldn't make out who he was speaking with; either Tom or Steve but it had to be one of them.

"I'm working from home today. Nothing is too pressing, other than what Selina discovered with the rig. Let's get a construction team out there to figure out what we can do and see if we can get a relocation plan in place for it too."

It was quiet as Damien must have been listening to the conversation.

"I don't care Tom. I'll handle my Dad and he can handle the board. There is nothing wrong with what goes on in our private lives. It's none of their fucking business. I'll talk to you later." Hearing the phone slamming on the counter, I walked into the room watching Damien gripping the counter in anger.

"Damien?" I held his bathrobe tighter around me as I looked at him. I was so afraid of what I would see in his eyes. Would he regret getting involved with me? If it meant his job, it would kill me but I would walk away.

"Come here Selina." He had his arms opened to me as I stepped into them. Feeling him hug me tightly to him, he rested his chin on top of my head.

"There seems to be a problem if you and I have a relationship. The Board doesn't believe in fraternization between employees. I've already told my Dad to go screw himself until he then spoke to me as his Dad. Then I received his blessing. We are going to have to be really careful unless we want a serious problem."

As I listened to him, I had tears in my eyes. I finally find a chance for happiness and a group of ten men might be standing in our way, including Damien's Father. As much as it killed me to say this to Damien, I found the courage.

"Listen, if this is going to mean your job, I can't let that happen. I won't let you sacrifice your life's work for me, for us. I will leave so you can continue on."

By the time I finished what I needed to say, I tried to keep the tears at bay but they trickled down my cheeks.

"There is no way in Hell I will ever let you go or have you give up on us. We will find a way to be together. I won't let anyone dictate what we can or can't do. Do you understand me?"

Nodding my head as I couldn't trust myself to speak, Damien ordered me to get dressed as we were going for a drive. As I got ready, I heard him call for the Corvette. Hurrying as to not keep him waiting, I was ready in record time. Grabbing an apple from the fridge, I grabbed my sunglasses and handbag to enjoy the day with my love.

As Damien drove thru the winding roads, he seemed to be lost in thought. Once in a while, he turned his head to smile at me but kept his concentration on the road ahead. Pulling off to the side of the road, he got out of the car and came around to open the door to help me out.

"I'm sorry that I haven't been talking on this ride. I do a lot of problem solving as I drive around."

He leaned up against the side of the car and pulled me between his legs.

"This is what we can do. It's the only solution I can think of that the Board can't do anything about. We can get married."

"What? Get married! Damien, I just met you a week ago."

"Yes and almost got killed twice, we had sex plenty of times, including had some fun on the plane ride here. There has been a lot of firsts in a week's time."

"I don't know Damien, this is too soon. I don't even know your favorite color."

"I have two actually, red and black, but I'm being serious."

"So am I. I think we should just be careful and revisit this idea of yours six months down the road."

"I will never give you up. You are mine Selina and no one is going to decide that for me but me. Do you understand that?"

"Yes, I understand."

"Ok, so tomorrow, we will both be in the office. We won't be seen together without someone with us. We will go to work separately and leave separately. We won't give anyone any reason to gossip about us to anyone. Understand?"

"Yes Sir."

"Good girl. We will have to be careful about each other's homes too. There are security cameras in both."

"This is horrible, we are grown adults and trying to sneak around."

"I think I can ask my brother and sister for help here. Actually my sister has a separate house on her property that I'm sure she will allow us to use it."

"Our own Love Shack," giggled Selina.

"I guess you can call it that. I'll call her tonight and explain the situation. She will have to keep her mouth shut around Dad and also my Mom, but I think it can work. Also, use your personal phone to contact me. You already have my number for my personal line. Stay off the business phone to speak to me."

"Ok Damien, we will try this. But if any trouble comes of this, we will have to make another decision and it's one that I'll make so I don't stand in your way."

"Don't say it Selina. I'm hoping if something happens, it's after this six month mark. Now let's get back so I can get you back to your place. It's going to be a long tiresome six months."

We seem to be satisfied with the plan in place. We got back to Damien's as I packed up my things. He called DT to come pick me up as we needed to put up the false pretenses immediately.

Unfortunately, DT was his efficient self and was in front of the building in ten minutes. Kissing Damien, I held back tears that made my eyes look like topaz gems.

"It will be fine Selina. Don't worry."

Making my way down the elevator, I just leaned against the wall as I hugged my overnight bag to myself. How were we ever going to pull this off?

Chapter 33 Game is in place

"Good morning Dr. Harrison." Damien reached over to grab a cup of coffee. He had Tom with him. Both of them winked at me.

"Good morning Gentlemen." Tom asked me how I was feeling after the ordeal I went thru this week. He reminded me that the wives are expecting me to go shopping with them on Saturday. I didn't forget. I was looking forward to female companionship and to get advice.

"Well, I have work to do. I'll have that report on your desk at the end of the day Mr. Stone."

"Wonderful Doctor. I appreciate it." Walking back to my desk, I saw several people looking at the three of us, trying to gage what we were speaking about. Calling Mike into my office, I had the charts laid out all over my work table.

"Doc, how are you feeling?"

"Very good Mike. It was incredible that this happened to me but the people are behind bars and life goes on, right?"

"I'm glad you are ok. Now what are we going to work on?"

For the rest of the afternoon, we finished mapping out the floor of the Gulf area in question as well as my take on the rig damage and the costs of relocating. The amount of money was staggering to do this project but compared to the disaster it could cause not to mention the incredibly negative press, the money was worth it.

Giving Mike everything for typing up the report, he got busy to finish it up by 5pm. The thought of a long and lonely night loomed ahead of me. How would we get to know each other if we couldn't be together to share our thoughts, dreams and ideas? God give me strength to get thru these months. I could end it all by saying yes to marriage. BUT I don't know him. Sexually, we are very compatible.

What about everything else that goes into a relationship? It isn't all about sex.
Hearing my text ring, I see that it's Julia.

Hey girl. What's up in Houston?

You wouldn't believe it if I told you.

Well, I know about the diving accident. Don't tell me something else happened? Did you marry that gorgeous hunk of a Boss?

No, not yet. It's complicated. I was almost a victim of his insane ex girlfriend and spent the night having mind blowing sex with him.

Ok, we have to Skype. You free tonight?

Yep, bring the wine. You are going to need it.

Will do my friend. I'll contact you say about 8pm?

Yes, that will work. Thank you for always being

there for me.

What would I do without Julia? So at least I have that to look forward to.

Hearing the buzzer on my desk phone, it was Mike. "Are you in for Denise?"

"I'll take it. Thank you Mike." Clicking over to pick up Denise's line, I was so happy to hear from her. It seems that Steve filled her in on everything that happened over the last 24 hours.

"Yes, I'm doing so much better Denise. It was crazy and I feel sorry for her as she has serious problems. Thank God she didn't do anything to me or to Damien."

"Therese and I are all up to speed on the guy's version of the story. It's incredible. I can't believe these things are happening to the both of you. We can talk over lunch on Saturday. We are still on for shopping, right?"

"Absolutely. I'm looking forward to it. I need to get back to normal living." As I was saying goodnight to her, Mike came into the office with the report all set, even with a cover on it.

"You make us look good Mike. Now do me a favor and bring it down to Anna. I'm going to pack up here and head out for the evening. You can leave too after you bring the report to her."

"Are you sure? I thought you might want to go over it with Mr. Stone."

"Not necessary," I said to him as I put my laptop into my briefcase. If this was going to work, I would have to be actress of the year. "If he has any questions, he will email or text. Have a great weekend Mike. God knows we both need it."

"Good night Doc." I caught him frowning at me as he left the room. I'm sure he thinks it strange that I didn't go see Damien but I can't without raising red flags all over the office. Pushing back the melancholy feeling that was creeping over me, I grabbed my computer bag and handbag, shut off the light and headed out to my car.

Hearing my private phone buzz, I saw that a text came in from Damien.

I just saw you leave the building. Thank you for the report. Anna just gave it to me. So professional looking.

You can thank Mike for that. He is a wonderful employee. You are very lucky to have him.

I'll make sure to note that with HR and have that put in his file. Are you ok?

As best as I can be under the circumstances. You?

The same. But we'll figure this out. I promise you.

I know.

What are you doing tonight?

Skyping with Julia. She wants to get up to speed on everything. I'll give her the PG version. LOL

I appreciate that. LOL Invite her to come here, I would love to meet her.

Let's see how she is after we drink wine together tonight and I fill her in on things.

She's a good friend.

Yes, a sister from another Mister. I'll call you later, ok?

Sure Princess. Drive safe.

Putting my car in drive, I headed back to my apartment with a million thoughts going thru my head about Damien.

Chapter 34 The Gathering

Ok Sel. You have two ways of getting thru this. You follow the plan that Damien laid out: hopefully his sister will cooperate and lend you her cottage house for your sexy liaisons or you can pack it up and high tail it back to Jersey. The way I see it, you should take your chances of happiness and sneak around for 6 months or so, get to know each other and have that ring slammed on your finger. In the meantime, you do an amazing job at the company that those crusty old men fall in love with the idea of you and Damien in love. Really, this is an antiquated idea that they all have. So what do you think?

I love him. I can't give him up, that's what my heart tells me. My head, that scientific part of me is analyzing everything. How can one analyze their feelings like I approach things? It's not normal.

No it's not. Listen, you have a chance for real happiness with a great guy. Spend time with him, be careful not to be alone with him at work to throw the old geezers off the trail and just enjoy yourselves with pure hot sex and love. Geez, I hate you. Maybe I should come to Houston and find me a guy. This Jersey scene is not happening for me.

Well, I was going to ask you to come on down, even if for a long weekend. Damien said he would love to meet you. AND just maybe he might have someone for you. What do you say?

I don't know if I can. My business is taking off now; I don't want to leave it mid-stride with a few associates holding down the fort. Let me think about this and get back to you. In the meantime, don't think about this too much and live Sel. We get one life, no regrets, OK?

Yes Jules. Thank you so much. I don't know what I would do without you.

Yes you do. You will have Damien to help you with everything. Just make sure I'm your Maid of Honor when the time comes.

Oh that's such a given. I love you.

I love you too Sel.   Good night.

As we signed off from Skype, I sat there thinking about my friend. I counted myself a lucky girl to have Julia in my life, a girlfriend I could share everything with. I don't know many people that have this gift. She was the best.

Picking up the phone, I called Damien. Just hearing his voice when he picked up the phone gave me the chills.

"Hey Princess. How was the Skype call?"

"You don't forget anything, do you?"

"Not when it pertains to you, I don't. I was reading over the report just a few minutes ago. So you think moving the rig is going to do the trick? It's an expensive effort but if that's your recommendation, I'll let the Board know."

"I know it's the safest and it won't interfere with drilling. The oil is still there, quite a vast amount too. And the rig needs to be repaired too, don't forget that."

"Definitely. Now onto other things. I spoke to my sister. The cottage is ours. She already fixed it up

and hired a service to come in and clean it up. So
what do you say about this weekend?"

"Yes, let's do this."

"Ok, I won't be able to pick you up for the obvious
reasons so let's meet tomorrow morning at the
grocery store at 9. We can pick up some things
and then you can follow me. Once you know how
to get to the cottage, you will just be able to go
there. We'll park behind the house too so no one
will see the cars once we are there."

"That sounds great Damien. I can't wait to see
you."

Over the next hour, we talked about our families. I
laughed out loud at the antics that Damien pulled
with his brother on their sister. No wonder Dawn
had to be tough. I talked about the digs I went on
with my Dad and the competitions I went to when
my brother competed with his body building. It
was just nice to be able to get to know more about
him besides his favorite colors. Before we knew it,
an hour went by and the wine was making me
sleepy. Being kept up most of the night before
didn't help either. Not being able to keep the
yawns to myself, Damien wished me a good night

and that he would see me in the morning. I just hugged myself after hanging up with him. This could just work. Time would tell.

Chapter 35 The Love Shack

It was lovely. Going down the drive, Dawn waved to both of us but gave us our privacy. I figured we would see her later on so I could thank her for helping us find a way to be together.

Reaching into my trunk for my overnight bag and laptop, I felt arms of steel wrap themselves around me as lips caressed my neck. Dropping my bags back in the trunk, I turned myself around in his arms.

"Hmm Mr. Stone. I like what you do to me." Pulling me closer to him, his mouth ravaged mine with a hunger that I felt right down to my toes. It was almost desperate, like he was afraid that this wasn't going to work and I would disappear. I told you I over think things. Lifting my hands thru his thick hair, I pulled myself closer to him. I needed Damien right now.

"To Hell with the bags, they can wait. I can't."

Slamming the trunk down, he picked me up like I weighed five pounds and pushed the door open. His sister left it unlocked for us. Thank God as he would have gone right thru the lock. As I wrapped my legs around his waist, he walked right into the bedroom and dropped me on the bed.

"Take off your jeans and top," ordered Damien. I liked his side of him. I'm always so in control of everything in my life, it was nice to have him be in charge of this.

He didn't take his eyes off of me when he took off his own jeans and top. Standing in his sexy briefs with evidence of his desire pushing against them, I couldn't help but lick my lips when I stared at him.

"Come here Selina."

He didn't need to ask me twice as I melted into his arms. His mouth descended on my lips as his tongue danced with mine. Biting my lips, I couldn't help but moan into his mouth.

"You like that don't you my baby?"

I couldn't even speak so I just nodded my head. He firmly pulled my hair back so my neck was tilted to the side. He placed his lips there and worked his way down my neck until he put his lips onto my nipple. I didn't even realize when he took my bra off. Such a smooth move Mr. Stone.

I was losing it. The sensations he was causing inside of me were building with each kiss, bite and touch. He knew what made me tick already. Hearing a tear of fabric, I realized he ripped my thong off my body. Looking up at me, he gave me a slight smile.

"I saved myself some time. I'll buy you a dozen."

I couldn't help but giggle until I felt him part my folds with his fingers and put his mouth right onto my clit.

"Jesus Damien, what you do to me!"

"We are just getting started sweetheart."

I was glad he was holding me up as I would have fallen down. Damien moved his tongue between my folds as he pushed his fingers inside of me. Hearing sounds in the room, I realized it was me. As he moved his fingers, he found the spot that sent me over the edge.

"Damien, please, faster," I cried as I pulled his head closer into me. I was on fire. Screaming his name, I fell over the edge as Damien watched me in my passion.

"You are so beautiful Selina. Come for me baby."
As the waves of desire kept coming, I was overcome with the beauty of it that I started collapsing on top of him.

"Hang on baby. We aren't done yet."
Picking me up, Damien fell on top of me in the bed and impaled me with one movement. I arched my back up to him from how sensitive I was. Moving fast inside of me, Damien held my head and looked deep into my eyes.

"Look at me Selina, I want to watch you come again in my arms."
I don't know how this would be possible but I felt the familiar build up happening again. He knew exactly what I needed and how to get me there. Staring into those blue eyes, I was lost and totally in love with this man.

"You feel so good baby. I can't get enough of you."
I couldn't help but close my eyes to the feelings that were building inside of me.

"Eyes. On. Me!" Demanded Damien.
Moving faster inside of me, I knew he was near. The desperation to share this together was

reaching its peak.

"Damien, I'm going to come."

I grabbed his strong arms as his fingers pulled at my nipples.

"Yes, Damien." I knew I was gripping his cock from the magnitude of my orgasm. Pushing himself harder, he joined me, locking eyes with mine and sharing all of his love with me. Crashing his lips on mine, I wrapped my legs around his waist and milked everything out of him. Hearing him groan into my mouth gave me a sense of satisfaction that I pleased my man. There is nothing like that feeling, especially if he's the man that you love. Wiping his forehead while moving his hair off his forehead, he gave me that high wattage smile while he put his forehead onto mine.

"God Princess, you are incredible." Placing kisses all over his face, he lovingly touched my cheek and softly kissed my mouth. Pulling out of me left such an empty feeling. I hated this but knew there would be more where this came from. Cradling me in his arms, he kissed the top of my head and pulled me closer to him.

"You know I'm going to owe my sister big time."

I just started laughing, thinking of the same thing.
"Yes, you are. But anything is worth it to be here with you."

"I'm going to so enjoy this weekend with you."
And so we did. We spent the time getting to know each other, enjoyed more time in bed together and just called his sister instead of going to see her. We didn't want to share any precious time that we had this weekend with anyone else. Until we got past that part of the relationship, we kept to ourselves and hid our relationship from everyone. Weeks turned into months and so far so good. It seemed like the heat was off of us. No one saw us together by ourselves. We always had Tom or Steve with us. I would spend some time with Denise and Therese and enjoyed my shopping sprees with them. One time, I ended up buying a dozen pairs of thongs. Denise had given me an eyebrow raise as to question why so many pairs.

"I don't want to know," she laughed at the checkout register.

It was just going well. The rig was moved successfully and the drilling commenced. Stone Oil was a pioneer in the practices of drilling that other companies were now following suit. I was being paid for my consulting work with the other companies too. Damien encouraged that process and knew that I was valuable not just to Stone Industries but to any other Houston company that wanted to step up to set higher standards. It was a dream come true for me to make a difference. We were getting closer in our relationship, stealing away on the weekends to our "love shack". We got to really know each other, what our dreams were and that we wanted to share a life together. I love Damien; I had no doubt about that. I just didn't know what we were going to do about it. Damien hadn't said anything else about our future so maybe he was happy with things the way there were. I was for the time being but knew that I would definitely want something more permanent in my life. I only hoped he felt the same way. Everything that we wanted to do was happening. It just felt too good to be true. I was so anxious that something else was going to happen. And then it did.

Chapter 36 Damien: The Gala

"Hello Dad. You are here early. Is there anything wrong?"

"No Son. I'm just coming in to talk to you about the Gala coming up. You know how important it is to the State that all of the oil companies are represented."

"Yes, I'm aware and we will be there as the sponsor of the event. Why the sudden interest in it?"

"Well, I spoke with our competitor in Dallas. Remember MacKenzie Oil, Stanton MacKenzie to be exact? He has a beautiful daughter that is his VP who needs a date that night. So in order to keep some kind of peace between our companies, we both thought it would be perfect for you to be her date for the evening."

"Dad, are you serious? Isn't this a bit old fashioned, trying to set up your son with another oil companies daughter? The answer is no."

"Damien, you aren't seeing anyone, you haven't said anything about Selina so I figured that there wasn't an issue here. You should be seen with someone at the Gala and what better person to have on your arm but Ms. MacKenzie."

This was totally out of control and wasn't going to happen.

"How do you know there isn't something happening with Selina? The answer is no."

"It's done Son. We are working out the joint sharing of the drilling with Mackenzie. This one gesture cements our working relationship and if it grows into something else, then it's so much better for both companies."

"Dad, I need you to leave my office right now. I'm not having this discussion with you any longer."

"Ok Son. Ms. Mackenzie will be calling you today to finalize the plans. She is a very straightforward young woman. I'm sure she will meet you at the Gala as it's her plan."

As his Dad walked out of Damien's office, Damien didn't see the smile on his face.

This is a fucked up situation. Now what do I tell Selina? It was bad enough that I couldn't go with her in the first place and now I have to be seen with another woman on my arm. And who's to say Selina won't have someone take her now in retaliation. My girl did have a short temper at times and this is going to be one of those times. Picking up my cell, I sent Selina a quick message.

Can you meet me at the shack tonight?

Sure. What's the matter; can't get enough of me?

Yeah, something like that.

I'll see you there love.

See you later.

Ok, Selina seems like she is in a good mood. I dread telling her. Hearing my phone ring, Anna said that a Ms. Mackenzie was on the line. Telling her to put her through, I braced myself for the drama to start.

"Ms. Mackenzie, so nice of you to call me."

"Mr. Stone, it's so nice of you to escort me to the Gala. I have to say it's so unexpected, being that our companies are rivals. This would be a good show of unity between us, don't you think?"

"It serves a purpose, yes I agree."

"More than you can possibly know Damien. I can

call you that, right? Please call me Charlotte or Charlie for short."

"Yes, that's fine Charlie. Damien is fine."

"Listen, I'm going to be blunt with you and my father will absolutely kill me for telling you this. Ok, this was all cooked up by my father to show face for his company. You see, I'm a Lesbian and I can't be seen with my girlfriend in public, not only with this company but especially at the Gala. He's not ashamed of me but knows how people can be. All I want is to be with her and her with me but we can't." I couldn't help myself but I just started laughing out loud.

"Excuse me Charlie for laughing but this is so ironic. See I have the same problem but with my Geologist. I can't be seen with her because of the Board and certainly can't be seen with her in public. We have been secretly meeting every weekend at my sister's cottage, basically hiding away from everyone's eyes. When my Father came in this morning and told me that you are my date, well, let's just say I'm going thru the same problems as you and your partner. I have to tell Selina tonight that I have a date and it's not going to go over well at all."

"Wow Damien. It doesn't matter what our preferences are, we are both stuck in our business worlds. So let's put up a front together for this night. Wait, Selina Harrison is your girlfriend? She's a brilliant lady and so sexy too."

"And she's all mine too Charlie." We both instantly warmed to each other. I liked her already. Then I had a brilliant idea.

"You know Charlie, I have an idea for that night. Do you want to help me with it? It will be a way for you and your partner to be together at the Gala. I don't plan on being away from Selina more than I have to."

"Absolutely. What do I have to do?"

Later on at the cottage, Selina was in full rage. "You have got to be kidding me! Didn't you tell your Dad about us then? How could you do this to us and to me? My parents are coming to town with my brother. And you have no idea how Sean Jr. gets when he feels like I'm being mistreated. Oh my God, this is such a fucked up nightmare."

Then Selina broke out into some Spanish which I assumed were a string of curse words. I was glad I didn't know what she was saying. Running out of the room, she slammed the bedroom door in my face and locked it. Jesus, this didn't go well.

"Selina, open the door now."

"Go away Damien and shove your Neanderthal attitude up your ass. You should have told your Dad finally about us this morning. What do you think I am? Someone that you can fuck and that's it?"

"I'm not doing this with a door between us. Either open it up or I'm going to thru it."

"Go away Damien. I have nothing to say to you right now." That was it. Not only did she have a temper but so did I too. Shoving the door with all my weight, the lock gave way as the door slammed opened.

"So this is our first fight, let's have it." I walked right over to her as she stood her ground. She definitely wasn't going to back down. I knew that I hurt her. Then I saw tears gather in her topaz eyes; that was something I couldn't bear to see but I wanted her to open up to me before my emotions took over.

"Let's go Selina, tell me."

"This is all catching up to me. I want to shout it out that I love you but I can't. We have to sneak around like teenagers when we are adults that have proved that being partners has not interfered with our work ethics. I don't know how much longer I can do this Damien. It's not fair and not right." Selina put her face in her hands as she started crying out her frustration.

Folding her in my arms, I let her cry until the sobs subsided.

Looking up at me, I brought my lips down to hers. Grabbing her full bottom lip, I sucked on it until she opened up her mouth to let me in. Holding her curves against me, I made sure that she felt the evidence of my love for her too. All of a sudden, Selina moved away from me.

"I have to go Damien. I can't do this. I love you but I can't have a few stolen kisses, a quick feel and then" that" as we sneak around. I have to be by myself right now." Letting her go, I heard her crying as she left the cottage. This is just a mess but I knew she needed her space. I decided it was time I go to see my parents and let them know what is going on before I really lose her.

Hearing Selina's car pulling out of the driveway, I went to tell my sister that I owe her a door and hinge. Letting her know what had happened and what Dad did, Dawn agreed that I needed to go see our parents. I tried Selina's cell several times and it just went to voicemail. Shit, this isn't good. It's time to fight for us and to Hell with my position in the company. If they feel I can't do my job because I'm in love with our Geologist, then they can go fuck themselves. I am not going to give up the only happiness I could have in my life with this woman for my position in the company. I didn't need the job. I could leave now and live comfortably with Selina for the rest of our lives. If I could have both worlds, that would be perfect. But if I couldn't, I would walk away from Stone Oil Industries for that woman and not look back. The realization of this decision rocked me. For so many years, Stone Oil was my life, was everything to me. Now I knew I was in love with Selina Harrison and nothing and no one was going to stop me.

Driving over to my parents, I saw that both their cars were in the driveway. Walking in, I called out to the both of them.

"We are in the kitchen Damien." Mom jumped up to give me a hug and then stepped back to look at me.

"What's wrong Damien?"

"Sit Mom, I want to talk to both of you." Watching Mom sit next to my Dad, she held onto his hand as she braced herself for what I needed to tell them. I grabbed a bottle of water and settled into the seat in front of them and proceeded to tell them everything. I told them about the dive to the hospital, to Lauren, to meeting each other secretly at Dawn's cottage for the past five months. I told Mom about the "date" Dad set up and that Charlie was a Lesbian and in the same position as I was with work and Selina.

"Do you love her Son?"

"Yeah Pop, I do."

"So what are you going to do about it?"

I smiled at my folks as my Mom had tears in her eyes. Dad decided to set things straight with me. "Damien, the Board will get over it. Winston suspected something between the two of you. He is so in love with Selina and the money she has made him with her advisements, I don't think there will be any problems now with any of them. And if there is, I will handle it for you. The most important thing is to be happy. Most people get one chance in life to find true happiness and love. If Selina is the one for you, then who are we to stand in your way Son? I have to admit, I knew that something was going on with Selina. You have been absent on the weekends and we knew it was a matter of time before you told us what was going on. Your sister let things slip one day about opening up the cottage. We kind of put two and two together."

"That's Dawn for you. She can't keep her damn mouth shut." After a good laugh and really feeling a tremendous weight lifted off of my shoulders, I looked over at my Mom.

"Mom, are you ok?" Seeing my Dad put his arm around her, she smiled over at me.

"I love that girl Damien. She is perfect for you and I know you will both be very happy together. Right now, she is hurting and you have to fix this, ok? Don't lose her over your job."

Getting up to hug my Mom, I realized how

important it was to fight for and keep the person that makes your life complete. Hugging my Dad next, I had to put my plan in action.

Chapter 37: Plan in Motion

While Selina ignored my calls, I knew I had to make an important move. Dialing her parents in New Jersey, a gruff voice answered on the other end.
"Harrison residence."
"Dr. Harrison please."
"Yeah, who's calling?"
"Damien Stone."
"Ah, Stone. This is Sean Harrison Jr, Selina's brother. What can I do for you?"
Hearing the protective tone of his voice, Selina wasn't kidding when it came to the both of them.
"Hello Mr. Harrison, I was wondering if your Father was available so I could speak to him."
Hearing Sean Jr. call out to his Father, he told him that the call was for him.
"It's Damien Stone for you Dad." Hearing an answer, Sean Jr. came back on the line.
"Hang on, my Father will come to the phone.

Better make it good Stone. Whatever it is you want to speak to my Dad about, you better do the right thing."

"Not to worry Sean. I've got this." Hearing a chuckle from the other end, I heard him tell his Dad to brace himself.

"Hello Mr. Stone, how are you?"

"I'm well Dr. Harrison and please call me Damien."

"Very well Damien. Is everything ok with Selina?"

"Well Sir, not really, I've messed things up a bit." I went thru the whole story with him. I left out some of the things that Father's shouldn't know about but definitely acknowledged the mistake I made by not stepping up to the Board, declaring my love for her and dealing with the consequences.

"The bottom line is that I love your daughter Sir and I want to spend the rest of my life with her. I'm asking you, your wife and son if I may ask her to marry me. I promise to take care of her, love and protect her. She's my life Dr. Harrison."

Little did I know that Dr. Harrison had me on speaker phone so Selina's mom and brother heard the story. Sean Jr. was the first to speak up.

"You did the right thing Stone. Thank you."

"Damien, I'm so happy to call you my son. I knew my baby girl would find a new love in Houston," said Selina's mom.

"Well Son, it' a yes from all of us. We are coming in for the Gala too, all three of us. We can't wait to meet you tomorrow. Winston also reached out to me about attending as he loves Selina and wants to catch up on good times. Welcome to the family Damien."

"Thank you Sir. Now I have a plan in place and I will need all of your help. Selina isn't speaking to me right now and I have to ensure she will be at the Gala."

"You leave that to me," said Maria. "My daughter can be a bit stubborn but I'll take care of this."

"You have my help too Stone," said Sean Jr.

Letting them know my plan, I asked them to send me their flight arrivals so I can arrange the car pickup with DT. Everything was in place according to the plan. I just needed my Princess to be at the Gala.

Chapter 38 Selina: Stepping Away for my Sanity

Ok Jules, so now you have the whole story.

It's not over Selina. I think it's just beginning. So what if he has a date for that night. You should get one too and drive him crazy with jealously. You have to push him to stand up to whoever can block your happiness.

I can't live without him Jules. That much I know. The good thing is my parents and Sean Jr. will be here. You should come too. My brother always had a crush on you. That's why I think he hasn't had a serious relationship. He is pining away for you.

I love your brother. He's such a hunk and those muscles. Maybe I will come in tomorrow. Do you really think so? I mean about your brother and me? Do you think he really likes me?

Yep, for sure. More than likes you Jules. I know my brother. He just needs a little push in the right direction. It certainly is worth exploring.

Ok, let me look into flights and reach out to your mom. I'll be there tomorrow.

Bring a sexy floor length formal dress with you. It's a night to remember from what I hear.

You got it Sel. I can't wait to see you. Tell that hunky brother of yours I'm going to be there and he can be my date.

Oh he is going to die Jules. Will do. I'll see you this tomorrow.

At least I'll have my friend here for support while I watch Damien with another woman. How am I going to get thru tomorrow evening? I check my phone and it's loaded with texts and missed calls from Damien. I know if I hear his voice, I would end up in his arms and it will be the same thing all over again. Is this our existence? He has spoiled me for any other man. I'm only half existing without him. Feeling the tears of sadness and frustration fall down my face, I feel that this is a hopeless situation. Or should I just give in and keep things the way they are; destined to be his secret lover and nothing more.

Hearing my cell ring, I see that it's Damien. It's time I put my big girl pants on and talk to him.

"Hi."

"Hi Princess. Thank you for taking my call. I've been so worried about you."

"I kind of figured that. I've been angry at you. This whole situation is screwed up."

"Listen, let's wait until after the Gala tomorrow. I'm looking forward to meeting your parents and brother. Make sure I get their flight information so I can send DT over to pick them up. (I couldn't tell her that I had all of their flight information already because she will know I spoke to them and would want to know why.)

We will work this all out, I promise you. And you don't have to worry about my so called date tomorrow night. Her name is Charlie by the way."

"Why are you saying that I don't have to worry about her?"

"You are the only one that I will have eyes for tomorrow night. I'm sorry about everything but I promise to make it up to you."

"Damien, I just don't know how long I can do this."

"Not now Selina. Until tomorrow then. Get some rest."

"Good night Damien."

Ok, I'm having big time reservations about tomorrow night. I just don't know what I'm going to do with this situation. Deciding to call my parents, I was so happy to hear Sean Jr. answer the phone.

"Selina! How are you baby girl?"

"I'm well SJ. Hey listen, you have your tux for tomorrow night, right?"

"Yeah, all pressed and packed. If I make one wrong move in the damn thing, I'll look like the Hulk."

"I'm sure you will have all of Houston drooling over you. Well, I know one woman who will be."

Knowing that it's time to get that ball rolling, I decided to drop the bomb on my brother.

"Ok, what are you talking about?"

"Jules is coming in tomorrow too. Actually I told her you would be here and she jumped to make her flight reservation as she was Skyping with me."

"Jesus Sel. That woman drives me crazy, in a good way crazy."

"It's time you did something about it SJ. You guys are perfect for each other. She is a fitness buff like you, has a sick body. Actually, I hate the both of you."

"Hey Sel, I put you on a workout regimen to build up your muscle strength. You didn't do it. But really, you look great. Listen, Mom is trying to grab the phone from me."

"I need your flight info. Damien is sending his driver to pick all of you up."

"Get it from Mom. I have to run."

"Selina baby. I can't wait to see you tomorrow. Here is our flight information."

Then we spent the next half an hour catching up. I just love talking to her as she so lively and animated. They were looking forward to seeing Houston and meeting Damien. I didn't have the heart to tell her that things weren't that great with us right now and that we had to sneak around with our relationship. I know that wouldn't go over big with her so I just answered her questions and didn't go into too much detail. They would know soon enough when I went to the Gala with them and saw another woman on Damien's arm. I was afraid about my brother's response too but maybe with Julia here, she could distract him. Saying goodbye to her, I hung up and decided to get my gown out. Picking out my handbag and shoes, I placed everything to the side. I had the second bedroom all set for my parents. Sean Jr. would be on the couch and Julia said she already booked a room in the hotel nearby. She was hoping to get in some quality time with Sean and that wouldn't happen if she was staying with me. It seemed like everyone had to sneak around for love. Turning off the light, I made a promise to myself that I would accept for now what Damien could give me. And when I was ready, I would walk away from the both of us.

Chapter 39: Damien: The Gala

Now that I know that Selina's family was all settled into her condo, I jumped into the Corvette to go over to meet them. I didn't tell Selina I was coming as I wanted to surprise her too. I was a bit anxious in meeting them even though I told them the truth. I think it was everything catching up to me, to us. Cruising thru the streets in downtown Houston, I was able to unwind for a bit. I knew I was meeting her best friend Julia too. If she didn't like me, then I was done. The two girls were very close so I knew I had to turn up the charm. I'm sure she knows everything about how we met right up to our love shack rendezvous. It was time to face the music. So I got to the condo and parked out front. The security guard knows me so after a few casual words, he buzzed me up to her condo. Here goes nothing. Standing in front of the door, I hear laughter and excited voices coming from within. I had to bang on the door several times before Selina opened the door.

"Oh my God, Damien. This is a surprise."

I gathered her in my arms and kissed her, not like I wanted to, certainly not in front of her brother, but I missed her, A LOT.

Keeping my left arm around her waist, I introduced myself to her Dad, Mom, Julia and then her brother. Selina wasn't kidding when she said he was built like the Roc. I'm a pretty strong guy too but Sean Jr. wow. He could be the Roc's stunt double.

"It's so nice to finally meet Selina's family. I hope you had a good flight into town and DT took good care of you."

I made sure to keep Selina right next to me during

this exchange as she tried a little to move away from me. It wasn't going to happen.

"Yes, thank you Damien. Everything has been great and we love this place you have Selina set up in. Very beautiful and safe," said Dr. Harrison.

"We give only the best to our employees. We wanted to make sure that's it feels like home."

"How about a drink everyone?" Selina announced as she was able to pull away from me.

"I'll help you." This little minx wasn't getting away from me that easily. Into the kitchen I followed her, taking the glasses from the top cabinet as she couldn't reach it that easily.

Pulling her into my arms, I crushed her lips to mine. I couldn't help myself. It's been two days since I've seen her and that it wasn't acceptable to me. Hearing her soft moans, I knew that she wasn't indifferent to me either. She just tried to put up a good front. As Selina grabbed the front of my shirt, she pushed away from me.

"Please stop. If Sean Jr. comes in here, I don't know what he will do."

"I'll take my chances." Just at that moment, Sean Jr. stuck his head in the kitchen.

"Are we getting drinks or what?" Giving us both a wink, he went back out to Julia and my parents. I heard Julia tell him to leave us alone so now I know I have a good buffer with her here. Bringing out pitchers of lemonade and ice tea, we all sat around and caught up with each other. My parents got to know Damien and Julia kept winking at me. When Damien wasn't looking, she mouthed "Oh my God, He's Hot." I just rolled my eyes over at her. How old were we? We certainly weren't acting like mature woman.

"So what are you wearing to the Gala tonight my dear?" God bless my Dad to keep the conversation going. After the women let everyone know what color dresses we were wearing, Damien spoke about the Gala in general. He had a speech to give tonight about what Stone Industries was doing to pave the way to the future.

"You are giving a speech tonight?"

"Yes Selina. I'm going to cover the work you have done too and also what you have done for the competing oil companies. We have become the forefront to what the oil business is going to aspire to do. We have you to thank for this."

"I knew my daughter would do great things in her work. I'm proud of you baby."

"Thanks Daddy."

"Well, I have to get ready for tonight. It was nice finally meeting everyone and I'll see you this evening. Your table will be right up front next to mine and the Board."

"It was good to meet you too Damien. Happy to be a part of this," said Dr. Harrison.

"Walk with me Selina." I held her hand as I stood up towards the door.

"I'll see you tonight. I want a few dances with you, ok?"

"Yes Damien, unless my dance card gets filled up." I wrapped my arms around her waist.

"Let's make sure that my name is on the entire card, ok?" I brought my lips down to hers for a searing kiss that I wanted her to think about until she saw me that night. Feeling her sway closer to me, I had to break the kiss before it went a little too far with her family right in the next room.

"I'll see you tonight Princess." Giving me a wink, he was gone.

Walking back into the living room, everyone spoke

at once.

"Handsome man," "Excellent manners," "He's got it bad for you," "You have to marry that man." It's easy to figure out who said what with this bunch. I just flopped onto the couch and grabbed the pillow to my stomach.

"He's pretty amazing but I have to tell all of you something." I proceeded to tell them about our situation, leaving out the sexy hot times we were together. Julia knew the stories but my parents and brother didn't. When I was done, my Mom was the first to speak.

"Selina baby, please give this time. I know it will all work out. Do you think your Father and I had an easy time of things? My family didn't accept your Daddy at first. They thought I would marry my neighbor down the street, even trying to do an arranged marriage for me. We stayed strong together but didn't want to alienate our families as family is all one has. But I couldn't let them decide my happiness or our happiness. And now look at us. Two beautiful children, two successful careers and so much love. Look at him, it's still like we are on our honeymoon."

"Ok Mom, we don't need a visual over here."

"Oh hush Sean Jr. You can be as lucky as us if you decide on beautiful Julia. There, I said it. You are both beautiful together. What are you both waiting for?"

Julia pushed her shoulder into Sean Jr. as he looked down at her with that gorgeous smile of his. Oh they were definitely on their way to happiness.

"Regardless," said Mom. "Love will find a way; Love never fails if you put your trust in it. Remember that my baby. Men like Damien don't come often so you have to decide to be with him or live your life without him. There is no in between." I went over to hug my mom as the tears started falling. She just rocked me as she looked over at my Dad.

"Selina, everything will work out. Of this I have no doubt. We can all tell how he feels about you. Just give him time to work it out with the business, ok? Now dry the tears, you need to look your best tonight and we all have to get ready for this amazing party." Hugging my Dad too, it was great to have them all in town. I missed them all so much. Wiping my face, I decided to put my best self forward and to enjoy the evening, no matter what happened.

So a few hours later, we were all looking our best. Daddy and Sean Jr. were dressed in their Armani tuxedos. Mama was in a gorgeous sapphire blue floor length gown by Badgley Mischka, Julia in a black Oscar de la Renta gown and me in a darker champagne colored gown also by Badgley Mischka. It was beautifully made with a bodice that came off the shoulders and had a little train. My hair was all curls cascading down my back with it pulled up on the sides. With my tan and exotic coloring, this dress was the perfect match. I couldn't wait for Damien to see me though I don't know if I will even get a chance to dance with him tonight. Cinderella was going to the ball without her Prince. Oh well. It wouldn't be the first time.

Hearing security buzzing for us, I knew DT was downstairs to pick us up. So deciding to put on a happy face, the five of us headed downstairs to what I'm sure would be an interesting evening. Sean Jr. already said he would escort Julia and me into the Gala so I didn't have to walk in alone. For some strange reason, I would feel very uncomfortable walking into that place by myself. I felt a little anxious coupled with feeling resentment. I resented the fact that ten people were controlling my road to happiness and resentment that Damien didn't stand up to these people, including his Father. I was anxious because I couldn't share this wonderful evening for his company with him but had to sit on the sidelines and watch him several tables from mine. I was upset that he will have a gorgeous woman on his arms. We are not in the best place and who knows what can happen. I can't believe that Damien has given up on us but just maybe this Charlie will be a temptation he wouldn't be able to resist. Even before this evening started, I wish it was over.

Lost in my thoughts, I didn't notice that four sets of eyes were focused on me and that we pulled up to Symphony Hall. Had I noticed, I would have seen Sean Jr. winking at everyone with a silly smile on his face. I just noticed the amount of Paparazzi that were gathered on the stairs going into the Gala. I planned on just trying to sneak in with Sean

Jr, find out where I was sitting and head to the nearest bar. A drink would settle my nerves and numb my feelings. Well, that wasn't going to happen. Seems the photographers had lists and photos of everyone who was anyone and they classified me as "a someone." Just my luck. I grabbed onto Sean Jr's arm with Julia on the other side.

Walking a few feet ahead of me was the man of my life: Damien looked absolutely incredible in an Armani tuxedo with a stunning blonde on his arm: Ms. Charlie McKenzie. They look beautiful together, the perfect power couple. I wanted to look away but I couldn't. I just seemed to want to punish myself for how I acted earlier at the cottage and might have thrown away the only true happiness I have always dreamed about.

 As the cameras flashed in their faces, Damien said something to Charlie that made her laugh out loud and move closer to him. I heard the photographers yelling out "Are you guys a couple?", "When did you start dating", "If you get married, would your companies merge?" I fought to keep the tears from gathering in my eyes.

"Hey Sel, don't worry about those idiots. You know that man is so in love with you, don't you?" Looking up at my big brother, I gave him a watery smile. I couldn't answer as the lump in my throat wouldn't make that possible. Sean Jr. has always been my protector and my best friend. I just couldn't take two failed relationships in one year. I'm definitely feeling like a relationship demolition magnet.

My Daddy and Mama were next. Daddy was definitely a celebrity in his own way and the press was excited to know he was here. Mama was radiant on his arm. The press loved them.

Then it was our turn. Even though the press took photos of the three of us, they asked if they could just get me alone. Unbelievable: I just wanted to find my seat and not be in the spotlight.

"Dr. Harrison, give us a smile," "Gorgeous lady, look over here," and "There she is: the brains and beauty behind Stone Industries."

"Yes, she is," said Damien as he came to stand next to me. "I thought you would want a little company," he whispered in my ear. The camera flashes were going crazy now, especially when

Damien put his arm possessively around my waist and placed a kiss on my forehead.

"What are you doing," I whispered to him. Damien didn't have a chance to answer with the reporters yelling out to him.

"Mr. Stone, is this the woman of your dreams?"

"Hey Stone, don't let this one get away."

"I promise you guys, I won't. You have your photos now. Have a good night," said Damien and he escorted me into the hall.

Pulling me into a secluded area, he held my hands up to his lips and kissed them.

"You look stunning tonight Selina. Again, I'm sorry about all of this. I hope that you have forgiven me so I can have a dance with you tonight."

How could I stay mad at this man? Mad wasn't the right word; disappointed was more the way I felt. Touching his face, I gave him a slight smile and asked to be shown to my seat.

"You don't want to keep Ms. Mackenzie waiting; that would be rude of you."

Damien knew I was disappointed with this whole situation. Creating a scene about it wouldn't change things so he escorted me to his table to introduce me to Charlie. He excused himself to get us a few cocktails while I stayed behind to speak to Ms. Mackenzie.

"It's so nice to meet you Doctor Harrison. I'm sorry that we are both in positions that we don't care to be in."

"It's nice to meet you too but I don't quite understand what you mean by that statement."

"I'm sorry, Damien didn't tell you?"

"Tell me what?" Charlie didn't have a chance to answer as Damien came back with our drinks.

"Please take good care of him for me, ok?" Excusing myself, I kept my tears at bay. Reaching my table, my brother put his arm around me and guided me to my seat. Taking a good sip of my drink, Jules was right by my side.

"What happened over there?" Asked Jules.

"I was introduced to Charlie, she mentioned that she was sorry about the positions we were both placed in and when I asked her what she meant by that, Damien came back with my drink. She wasn't able to clarify what she meant by that statement. I asked her to take care of Damien but maybe I shouldn't have said that." I couldn't help but laugh as my own words. I basically gave her permission to take care of him as she saw fit. What an idiot I was!

I looked back over to his table and he was seated facing me. He gave me that knee weakening smile. I could just hit him. He was having a good ole time as I sat here miserable. Well, that ends right now. I will just have to show him that I'm having a good time without him.

Sean Jr. came back to our table with drinks for me and Julia. I'll down this second one quickly to take the edge off and then I can enjoy myself. Soon the dinner courses began. I have to admit that I started to enjoy the evening. It was wonderful to spend time with my family that I started to relax. Everything was perfect right down to the four course meal that was served. Even the band was wonderful. I've had several dances already from men in different departments at Stone. It gave me a little satisfaction seeing Damien's reaction to me dancing with them. He didn't like it, I could tell. His eyes were a stormy grey and the laughter left his face. I wasn't going to let an argument and a "Charlie" affect my time to have some fun. So I danced with every man that asked me too. I was getting a bit exhausted and thought maybe this little act of defiance was starting to wear me down. About the time I finished my dance with my assistant Mike, I knew I could relax. All I wanted to do was take off my shoes but that wasn't going to happen any time soon.

As I was escorted back to our table, I kissed Mike on the cheek to thank him for the dance. I noticed Winston Clooney over at our table having a great time with my Daddy. It was wonderful they could reconnect their friendship and share good times again.

"Ah Doctor, there you are. I was wondering if you would do me the honor of this next dance."

"It would be my pleasure." Winston extended his arm to me which I gladly took. Smiling up at him, I wondered if this dance had a motive to it and he didn't disappoint me.

"So Doctor, are you having a good time?"

"Yes Mr. Clooney, I am. Thank you."

"I have a funny feeling that you would be having a better time if you sitting with Damien at his table."

I felt my feet do a little stumble at his words.

"I don't exactly know what you mean Sir."

"Oh, I think you do. I've known Damien a long time Selina, since he was a young man to be exact, to know that he is quite smitten with you. Even now, he is shooting daggers at me with his eyes from across the room. In fact, I've seen you dancing most of the night away and he has been simmering at his table. You are both providing me with quite the entertainment this evening."

"I'm happy to oblige Mr. Clooney." I couldn't keep the smile out of my voice.

"He thinks that the both of you can keep things secret but actually, I love the thought that Damien settles down. I am hoping that you are the woman to do that for him."

"I really don't know what to say Mr. Clooney. I think that it's up to Damien to decide."

"What? Don't you have a say here?"

"If I may speak frankly, there is a matter of the Board and fraternizing with the staff."

"Oh don't worry about those old guys, including Damien's Dad. We are all romantics at heart. Granted we don't want this happening in the workplace but how can one control a wayward heart? Now my dear, you just keep doing the good work you are doing at Stone and let nature take its course. Right now, I see Damien heading straight for us. I have a feeling that he is going to claim you for the rest of this dance. Young men nowadays. They need to learn from us seasoned professionals."

"Excuse me Mr. Clooney, may I have this dance with the good Doctor?"

"Sure my boy. What took you so long?" Bowing to me, Mr. Clooney kissed the back of my hand. "Remember what I told you. Enjoy the rest of your evening."

Damien didn't waste any time with pulling me close to his body.

"I have been waiting all night to dance with you Selina. It's driving me crazy seeing you out here with everyone but me."

"You haven't been sitting by yourself either Damien, not that I'm counting. Your "dance card" has been quite full too."

"You are the only one I want on that damned so called "dance card." You have been avoiding me."

"I didn't want to cause any gossip or problems for

you but I think that it doesn't matter any longer."

"What did Clooney talk to you about? You both looked really friendly."

"He asked about us and our relationship. Told me not to worry about the old men on the board either."

"Hmm interesting." Damien rested his head close to mine. "You know, you are driving me crazy in this dress and how you look. You look stunning. I want nothing more than to take you home with me and get started on more interesting things with you." I sensed that he wanted to say something else to me but the lights flickered a few times as the band ended their song. I saw Damien's Dad up on the stage to start the program.

"I have to get up there Princess. Let me take you back to your seat but at my table."

Damien escorted me right to the seat next to Charlie. Kissing me on the forehead, he headed up to the stage to stand next to his Dad.

As Charlie acknowledged me, I saw her holding the hand of another beautiful woman seated next to her.

"Dr. Harrison, while you asked me to watch over

Damien for you, he wasn't the one that I wanted to keep an eye on. Let me introduce you to my girlfriend Stephania. Had you given him a chance to explain things to you, Damien would have alleviated quite a bit of heartache I could see you were going thru this evening."

I was speechless; I really didn't know what to say as Charlie thoroughly put me in my place. I didn't trust Damien and imagined all kinds of crazy things about him and Charlie. To say that I was a bit embarrassed was putting it mildly.

"I'm so sorry Ms. Mackenzie that I misjudged you being Damien's "date" tonight."

"Listen, no apology needed. We are both going thru the same fight with our jobs to hide our relationships. Well, tonight, that ends for us. I want people to know that I love this wonderful woman by my side and that it doesn't affect how I perform my job. If they have a problem with that, well, they can go fuck themselves."

"Such language Charlie," scolded Stephania.

"That's just the right attitude to take. I wonder if Damien can get to that decision."

"Oh I believe he has Doctor. Let's enjoy the

program, shall we?"

I didn't know what this program was going to be about other than knowing that Stone Industries paid a hefty amount as the sponsor of this event so they were the company that would be highlighted in tonight's program. Mr. Stone started talking about the history of Stone Industries with a power point presentation full of images flashing on the screen behind him; all photos from when they started the company until today. It was quite interesting to see all of the old photographs of Damien's Grandfather breaking ground for the new Headquarters and starting this empire that Damien now runs with an iron fist.

"And now, without further adieu, I would love to turn this presentation over to my son, the CEO of Stone Industries, Damien Stone."

I couldn't help but feel proud of Damien at this moment as the applause from the audience was quite boisterous; he commanded a presence, a strength that has taken Stone Industries to another level. Besides looking so handsome up there, I'm sure I wasn't the only woman in the room that was enamored of him. All I wanted to do was to apologize for my insecure behavior tonight. I wouldn't feel better until I had that chance.

"Good evening everyone and welcome to the Gala. Stone Industries is proud to be this year's sponsor of this event and hope that everyone is having a wonderful time." Looking over at me, he gave me a smile that warmed my heart towards him. I felt the disappointment melt away. I couldn't fight him or what we had together. I love him. That was it, plain and simple. Somewhere along the way, I fell head over heels in love with this dynamic man. From that fateful flight to now, I am his. I belong to him; he owns my heart. Now, I just have to make things right between us again. No matter what happens, I have to be a part of his life. I'll take whatever he can give me given his CEO position. It's better than nothing at all.

"Stone Industries has taken a lot of positive moves in the future of oil drilling in this country. We have made great strides in securing a better future for our planet as well as pushing for energy independence from the Middle East. It's time that we become more concerned over what faulty drilling can do to our environment and for our future generations. As you can see, we have made drastic changes in our policies and our approach to drilling in the Gulf that other oil companies, such as Mackenzie Oil, have also joined the ranks of clean oil drilling. Now in order for Stone Industries to have made such changes, we hired a brilliant Geologist, Dr. Selina Harrison. Dr. Harrison brought to our attention the problems that were at hand for Stone Industries and with her expertise and advice, those changes not only proved to be profitable but also fell into the category of what Stone Industries wanted to represent to the world. If I may, I would love to invite Dr. Harrison to please come up to the stage."

Hearing the applause, I looked at my Daddy. With tears in his eyes, he nodded his head and came around to escort me to the stage. I didn't understand why Damien would want to bring me up there. I could have just waved from my seat which would be been more than sufficient. I didn't need to be in the spotlight.

"I'm so proud of you Selina. You have finished what you wanted to accomplish and that was to make a difference. You have done well my daughter." Kissing me on the forehead, he saw that Damien was standing on the steps waiting for me. Then my Daddy did something a little unusual; He shook Damien's hand and then placed my hand in his. As I watched him walk away, Damien softly called my name to walk with him to the center of the stage. Something wasn't right here.

"Ladies and gentlemen, I would love to introduce to you, Dr. Selina Harrison and if she will have me, I would love to introduce her as my future wife." I just looked at Damien as the place erupted with cheers and clapping. I stood there frozen and in shock. I couldn't believe Damien just asked me to marry him in front of 300 people, including the Board of Directors. Oh My God! I looked to my parent's table and they were all standing up cheering too. Sean Jr. gave me a thumbs up as my Mama and Julia were crying. Looking back at Damien, he was down on one knee holding an open ring box with the most beautiful diamond ring. The look on this man's face was full of love and passion and to me was everything I had ever wanted in a man, lover and friend. From the plane ride right to now, Damien knew who he wanted and that was me.

"Princess, will you be my friend, my lover and my wife, forever. I loved you from the moment I saw you. I knew that I had to have you as mine. I want to build a life with you, have children with you, and grow old with you. My life is incomplete without you Selina. Will you marry me Princess?"

"Yes, Oh my God, yes Damien! I love you and want to be your wife."

Standing next to me, he placed the ring on my finger which was a perfect fit. The tears were streaming down my face as I couldn't believe this was happening.

Damien said into the microphone, "She said yes!" Hearing the cheers go up again, Damien held my face between his hands and just kissed me in front of all of those people. Neither of us cared at that point, it was just us, together. After all that we had endured in these short months, we knew that we were meant to be together. Turning towards the crowd, we saw Damien's parents with my parents. Our mom's were still crying tears of happiness and our Father's were shaking each other's hands. The Board members were all standing and applauding. Winston blew me a kiss with a wink that was so endearing that I blew a kiss right back to him. It seemed as though this Gala was turning out to be a huge engagement party now. Damien told the band to start playing as we exited off the stage to our families. I couldn't believe this had happened. The women wanted to see the ring while the men just slapped Damien on his back.

I heard Sean Jr. mention the Bachelor Party and that they should go to Vegas as he has good connections there. I just threw my napkin at him as Julia told him to knock it off.

"Can Sel at least wait until the ring is on her finger for at least 24 hours?" Julia scolded Sean Jr. as she came over to stand next to me.

"So my dear friend, this is your happy ending. I knew it wasn't over. What you don't know is that Damien had called your parents and SJ, explained everything that he could and left out the personal things. He asked them for your hand in marriage so we all knew this was going to happen tonight.

We just didn't know how he was going to do it. Damien is the one for you Sel. No doubt about it and I couldn't be happier for you and for him. Just remember, he has a great woman in you too. He's a lucky man."

"Yes, I am Jules. I'll remember that every day of my life," said Damien as he wrapped his arms around my waist as he stood behind me. Kissing my neck, I turned around and just smiled up at him. I knew at that moment, I would be protected, adored and just loved by this special man.

"I'm so sorry I doubted you and our argument and thinking you wanted to be with Charlie."

Putting his finger over my lips, he stopped me mid-sentence.

"I'm sorry for not doing this sooner."

"Thank you Damien for choosing me."

"No, thank you Princess for saying yes."

At that moment, I looked forward to our future and our happy ending.

Thank you's…..

"If Somebody Believes in You, and You Believe in Your Dreams, It Can Happen"

I hope you have enjoyed the love story of Damien and Selina as much as I have enjoyed writing this for you. There are a few people that I would love to thank as I go thru my journey with sharing these stories: (If I have forgotten anyone, please forgive me and let me know)

My husband Bobby: who is patient with me as I escape into this World of Romance, Love and Intrigue. He understands my creative side as I take time away from him to write these stories. He knows I'm in the house and never far from him.

My family: Mama, Dad and Sandy for their support and love. I'm sorry if I'm embarrassing my brothers with these stories ☺ They should know me by now.

Elizabeth, Ethan and Ryan, you two can read the stories when you are 25. ☺

Chrissie and Becky, my beautiful Step-Daughters, and the boys.

Aunt Gidget in Ohio: You are my biggest fan out there besides my Mama. Thank you for telling your friends about my books. I'll ask Grant and Kate to sign copies for you and your friends!

Jimmy Kimmel: people have asked me why I #Jimmy Kimmel: well he needs to put me on his show after my 5th release in Jan. 2017. ☺

Ahren Sanders and Julie Johnson: my writer "friends" who have given me guidelines and advice as I venture into this whole romance writing gig. I know I will meet them at some point.

My friends and FB friends for posting and reposting when I have a release coming out. It's all about Social Media now and I appreciate you spreading the word for me. (Melinda, Sonia, JD, Jamie, Earnest (Do you want to eat my Taters? Tater tots folks. It just came out all wrong over a client breakfast one morning. I have a way with words at times) Linda P, Danny P(the World Famous Potter and my publicity agent during our vacation at Emerald Isle, that is if you count yelling out my name up and down grocery aisles whenever he saw me pushing our cart. Gee, how glamorous am I. It was hysterical.) Elaine G, Nadine P, Topher, JD (it's her fault that I'm doing my writing now. I might owe her a vacation in the future LOL) To my furbabies: Rocky and Sammy, always near me while I work on the book unless Bobby is eating something in the den; that's when they will leave me. They are the sweetest pups on the planet to me.

<u>For my beautiful and wonderful cover Models</u>:

<u>The insanely handsome Grant Luther, Wilhelmina NY model/Fitness Division and my friend</u>: When I first met you, I knew you were Damien Stone and kind of blurted that out to you. ☺ You said you would be honored to be on my cover. I am honored that you are part of this as you made Damien come alive; not only for me but for anyone that reads this. I can't thank you enough fellow Aries.

The stunning Kate Johnson, Wilhelmina NY model/Direct Division: I have known and worked with Kate for at least 10 years. You are the perfect Selina! Sexy, strong with a bit of innocence. I knew once Grant agreed to do the cover, you would be his perfect Selina. You both created magic on set, it was infectious to watch. You are a living doll to have done this for me.

To the incredibly talented Michael Reh, Photographer and friend. You brought it all together. I showed you a few ideas that you took it to another level. Sexy but not over the top. That's what I envisioned and you delivered. You made this a lot of fun. Thank you!

Mariano, our assistant. You were wonderful to have on hand to do what assistant's do ☺ I listened when you said "You've got the shot." I so appreciated your help that day. Thank you!

<u>To Melissa at MG Book Covers</u>: Once again, a beautifully designed cover that exceeded all my expectations. Wow! You will have all of my covers! You are my book cover Guru!!

Thank you to the Bloggers, reviewers; your networking is so important for getting the word out for Independent Writers. I appreciate you! Thank you! Thank you!! Thank you!!!

<u>The Future:</u>

My next book, "Desire's Way" will be released in November.
"Second Chance at Love" will be released in January.
And I'm thinking of a sequel with this book ☺. I've also had requests for a sequel of "A Love in Name Only." You guys are going to keep the creative thoughts really busy! I hope I can keep up with your demands ☺
All of my books are available on Amazon.com under Ginni Conquest and in several languages too.

Contact:

www.Ginniconquest.com

Facebook: Ginni Conquest (Author Page)

Sweetandsexyromance1

Instagram: Gindoll1

email: Gindoll2005@yahoo.com

I would love to hear from you!

About:

Ginni Conquest started her Romance Writing last year with her first release "A Crime of the Heart" followed shortly by her paperback release "A Love in Name Only." She started out writing Children's books and has a collection entitled "The Adventures of Mac and Cletus," which are stories based around her two beloved Basset Hounds. Not getting the response she wanted for them, Ginni put aside writing until she had a dream that developed into a whole book:

"A Love in Name Only" was born and she hasn't looked back.

Living in New Jersey with her husband Bobby and their two Basset Hounds, Rocky and Sammy, Ginni still works full time in New York City while writing on her long commute as well as in her spare time some evenings and on the weekends. She loves motorcycle rides and plans to get her own license next year. She loves the Lake, the Beach, Date Nights with her man and just having fun. Life is too short not to enjoy it! Xxxxx

87236130R00148

Made in the USA
San Bernardino, CA
03 September 2018